D0015865

:3
+16
7
1989

PERRY MASON

IN

The Case of
Too Many Murders

PERRY MASON
IN
The Case of
Too Many Murders

Thomas Chastain

Based on characters created by
Erle Stanley Gardner

WILLIAM MORROW AND COMPANY, INC.
New York

PERRY MASON

IN

The Case of
Too Many Murders

1

"Hey! Look who just came in!"

Eddie Deegan, the bartender, nudged John Fallon, who was standing next to him behind the bar.

John Fallon, manager of the Oaks Restaurant, glanced at the door. The big man making his way into the room would never be inconspicuous, not with the shaggy gray hair, the gray beard, the Stetson hat pushed back on his head, and the tinted aviator sunglasses covering his eyes.

Fallon decided that even people who might not have seen all the pictures on the front pages of newspapers and on television in past weeks would have noticed Gil Adrian.

Later, at the trial, Fallon would testify: "The restaurant was practically full that night, and I saw that most of the other diners were watching him as he went to the phone booth, made a call, and then came back and sat at a table and ordered a drink. The time was close to nine P.M."

John Fallon had known Adrian long before the photographs and stories had appeared in newspapers and on television reporting that Gil Adrian had been indicted and was facing trial for allegedly bribing a dozen city and state politicians. Adrian, who had until then been a well-known and wealthy California businessman and real estate operator, also was reported to have ties with organized crime figures in the state and in Las Vegas, Nevada.

For several years, up until six months earlier, Gil Adrian and his wife, Laurel, had been regular customers at the Oaks Restaurant. Fallon had found out they lived not far away in the hills up above the restaurant. According to recent news accounts the couple were separated. Gil Adrian was reported to be involved in an affair with one of the city's councilwomen, Janet Coleman. It was rumored that City Councilwoman Coleman had interceded with the politicians Adrian had bribed in order to get favored city and state contracts for himself.

Knowing all this, Fallon was curious about whether Adrian would remain alone at the Oaks Restaurant or who might join him at his table. Busy as he was that night, with the restaurant crowded, Fallon still paused from time to time to look over to where Adrian was sitting. About a quarter of an hour after Adrian arrived, Fallon saw that he had been joined by another man.

The restaurant manager did not recognize the other man, who was dark-haired, of medium height, and heavyset. Fallon did notice, however, that the two men seemed to be having a serious conversation and then that Adrian paid the check for the drinks the two had had and they were leaving.

Fallon continued to watch them as they went toward the door, Adrian in front of the other man. The restaurant manager was about to turn away when he saw that the two men were scuffling in the doorway. Then he saw the gun suddenly appear in Adrian's hand, heard the shots, one right after the other, and watched as the man he didn't know went down, blocking the entrance, his body halfway in, halfway out, of the restaurant.

Diners in the room were screaming and scrambling for cover. Fallon saw that Adrian had disappeared out the door.

"Call the police!" Fallon yelled to Eddie Deegan. Fallon vaulted over the bar and ran to the man lying in the doorway. The man had been shot twice, in the chest and the head. Fallon was sure he was dead even though he did not touch the body.

Fallon heard a car engine racing and looked out beyond the

body in time to see a black Mercedes sedan roaring out of the restaurant parking lot, the car's spinning rear wheels sending up a swirl of gravel before the car disappeared up the road.

It was only a matter of minutes, less than ten, before the first patrol car, which had been cruising in the area, pulled up to the door of the Oaks Restaurant. One of the patrolmen quickly determined that the man who had been shot was dead.

The other patrolman used the police-car radio to report to the station house the details of the shooting given him by John Fallon, including the identity of Gil Adrian and the information that Adrian owned a house in the hills nearby.

Two police cars responded to look for Gil Adrian. Police had the address of his house. Lieutenant Frank Latham, Homicide, drove one of the cars. Other patrol cars and an ambulance were sent to the Oaks Restaurant.

The house Gil Adrian owned was set back off the road at the end of a driveway behind a screen of shrubs and trees. The two police cars, at the order of Lieutenant Latham, using his car radio, approached the house with their sirens off.

Two other cars, a black Mercedes sedan and a cream-colored Lincoln Continental, were parked by the side of the house.

As the two police cars pulled up in front of the house, the cars' headlights illuminated the figure of a woman hurrying away from the front of the house toward the Mercedes and Lincoln parked in the side driveway. Latham was out of the door of his unmarked car before it stopped moving.

"Stop!" he called to the woman. "Police! Stay where you are!"

The woman, startled, stopped and stood waiting as Latham walked toward her, followed by four uniformed patrolmen.

"What is it? What's wrong?" the woman asked.

Latham had his wallet out and showed her his shield. "We're looking for Gilbert Adrian."

"I'm Laurel Adrian," the woman said. "Mrs. Gilbert Adrian."

"Where's your husband?"

"I don't know. He may be in the house. That's his car there. I just got here myself."

"You were leaving the house," Latham pointed out.

"I just got here myself," the woman said again. "I parked my car and had started toward the house when I discovered I didn't have my door keys. I thought I'd dropped them in the car. I was on my way back to the car before I went inside—and then you arrived. What's this all about?"

Latham ignored the question. "So you don't know whether your husband's inside or not."

She shook her head. "No. Except his car's here."

"All right," Latham said. "Let's take a look for the keys."

Laurel Adrian led the way to the car, looked inside, and quickly held up the keys on a ring. Then she moved past the police officers and returned to the house. She unlocked the door and went inside. Latham and the patrolmen were close behind her.

There was a light on in the foyer and Laurel Adrian called out her husband's name several times. When there was no answer, she said, "Perhaps he's in the den." She pointed down the hall. "I think I see a light shining from under the door there."

Again, she led the way, opened the door to the den, and stepped back quickly, bumping into Lieutenant Latham. Latham pushed past her and went into the den. The light was on.

The leather armchair behind the desk was overturned. Gilbert Adrian lay on his back on the floor beside the desk. He was dead, with a bullet wound in the center of his forehead, another between his eyes. His Stetson hat rested on the floor next to him. His tinted aviator glasses had apparently been shot off by the bullet that had struck him between the eyes. The two halves of the glasses had fallen onto the floor.

Laurel Adrian gave a small, stifled cry and took a step backward.

A .38-caliber revolver lay on the desk on top of a stack of typewritten papers. There were other papers scattered across the top of the desk, some of them torn into bits and pieces. The wastepaper basket next to the desk was filled with torn scraps of paper. A passport, flipped open, showing Adrian's photograph, was lying near a corner of the desk.

On the wall directly behind the desk an oil painting, hung on hinges, had been swung aside. In place the painting would have concealed the steel safe built into the wall. The door to the safe was open and the safe was empty. There were also what looked like two bullet holes in the wall behind the desk.

Lieutenant Latham ordered one of the patrolmen to phone the

station house and request that the coroner be sent, along with the forensic team who would examine the murder scene for finger-prints and other evidence.

Latham then turned his attention to Adrian's wife. He ques-tioned her in the living room. Two uniformed patrolmen were present.

"You said you'd just arrived home. Where were you earlier this evening?"

"You know my husband? You know who he is?"

Latham nodded. "We're acquainted with his background."

"He phoned me this afternoon. He asked me to meet him at our beach house tonight at eight-thirty. We're separated, you know. I've been living here; he's been at the house in Malibu."

"Yes. Go on."

"I had dinner. Alone. And then I drove out to Malibu. About halfway there, I suddenly thought that his calling me might be some kind of a trick. So I stopped and used a pay phone to call the house in Malibu. There was no answer. Then I called here. The phone was picked up and, as soon as I spoke, the line was discon-nected. I know it had to be him. I drove back."

"Why did you suddenly think he might be trying to trick you?"

"Because," Laurel Adrian gave a shrug, "that's the way he often acted."

"Did he tell you why he wanted to see you at the beach house tonight?"

"He said, as I knew, his trial was to start tomorrow. He said there were some papers we both had to sign."

She appeared flustered. "How—how did you happen to appear here when you did?"

Before Latham could answer, one of the patrolmen who had remained in the den came into the room.

"Lieutenant, I think you'd better take a look at something."

Latham left Laurel alone for a brief time and then returned, asking her to come with him to the den.

Once there, Latham pointed to an open drawer in the desk. There was a .32-caliber revolver in the drawer. "Whose gun is this?"

"It's mine," Laurel said quickly. "It's registered to me. My husband bought it for me. I kept it there in the desk drawer."

"We're going to have to impound it."

Laurel nodded. "I'd forgotten it was even there."

Lieutenant Latham looked at the two patrolmen and then at Laurel. His brow was furrowed as he said, "We've met before, haven't we? That other homicide case some months ago, six months ago, when one of your neighbors was killed during a robbery?"

"The Burress house up the block," Laurel said. "The police questioned everyone on the block."

"Yes, of course," Latham said. "We talked to you and your husband. That was a break-in and murder. We never caught whoever did it."

"Could this have been the work of the same person?" Laurel asked.

"I don't know." Latham paused before he said, "Mrs. Adrian, I'm going to have to ask you to come to the station house with us. We'll need a signed statement from you."

"Yes," she said, "of course I'll go."

"And," Latham said carefully, "I have to advise you that you should have a lawyer present."

2

The court clerk's voice was loud in the crowded room: "Members of the jury, have you agreed upon a verdict?"

Perry Mason, at the defense table, glanced at his client. Arthur Simmons was staring intently at the foreman in the jury box, who answered, "We have."

"What is your verdict?" the clerk asked.

"We find the defendant, Arthur Simmons, not guilty."

There was the sound of cheers in the courtroom.

Arthur Simmons was trembling as he turned and grasped Perry Mason's hand. "Thank you, thank you, Mr. Mason," he managed to say before a throng of spectators surged forward from their seats, surrounding the two men. Arthur Simmons was swept away by his mother and girlfriend and an enthusiastic group of friends.

Della Street was there then, shaking Mason's hand as she whispered, "I hope you're as proud of yourself as I am of you."

Mason looked at his confidential secretary and shook his head in amusement, still smiling. "Knowing your predisposition in favor of me, I doubt that that would be possible. But, yes, I am a little proud."

He started to turn toward the defense table to pick up his briefcase. Della Street said, "Guess who's come seeking help?"

"Della, you know how full my schedule is—"

"Still, I think you'll want to see her," Della persisted. "Mrs. Gilbert Adrian."

Mason said quickly, "Take her to the office. I'll meet you there."

Della went away.

Mason had read all the news accounts of Gilbert Adrian's alleged acts of bribery and of his murder last night.

He stood for a moment looking around the now-deserted courtroom. He *was* pleased that today he had managed to win freedom for Arthur Simmons, a victim of a gross miscarriage of justice.

Simmons had been convicted of the murder of his ex-employer and sentenced to prison two years ago. Simmons had been convicted on the testimony of two other employees of the accounting firm where Simmons had worked until he was fired by his employer, Herbert Benton.

Benton had been strangled by a telephone cord in his office in the evening one day after Simmons had been discharged after twenty years of service to the accounting firm. The two witnesses were Benton's secretary, Alice Marshall, and another accountant of the firm, Robert Cullin. Both testified that Simmons had appeared at the office demanding to see Benton, who had agreed to talk to him.

Cullin testified that he himself had been leaving for the day when Simmons arrived and he had gone on his way.

Alice Marshall's testimony was that Simmons had gone into Benton's office, that the two men had been alone for a while, and that then she had heard a scuffle taking place in the office and a loud scream from Herbert Benton: "He's strangling me! He's killing me!" Alice Marshall had then called the security guard on the phone in the lobby of the building.

Cullin, who by that time had reached the lobby, returned with the security guard and they had found the victim with the telephone cord wrapped around his neck, the receiver dangling from the end of the line. Simmons was standing over Benton's body.

Arthur Simmons, on the stand, swore that Alice Marshall had telephoned him that day and told him that Benton wanted to talk to him and gave him a time for the appointment that evening. He had gone to the accounting firm, had seen no one about, and had entered Benton's office only to find him already dead.

Simmons further swore there was a witness who could clear him; that there had been a man in the elevator with him who had heard—just as Simmons had heard—a man's voice screaming: "He's strangling me! He's killing me!" when the elevator reached the floor where the accounting firm was located. According to Simmons, this witness had not gotten off the elevator, which had gone on to a higher floor. Simmons had given a description of the man but the police had never been able to find him or to find anyone who had ever seen him. The jury had found Arthur Simmons guilty of murder.

Mason had not been involved in the case at the time of the first trial. Later, from prison, Arthur Simmons had written asking Mason to help him appeal his sentence. Mason reviewed Simmons's case and decided it was worthy of further investigation.

Part of Mason's decision was based upon a preliminary investigation that found that in the years since Simmons had been sent to prison, Alice Marshall and Robert Cullin had married and Cullin now ran the accounting firm once headed by the dead man, Herbert Benton.

The lawyer had directed a team of private detectives to undertake a search for the missing witness. After two years the man had finally been discovered. He was a salesman working for an export company in the Far East. On the night of the murder he had made a visit, without an appointment, on a possible client in the same building as the accounting firm. There was no one in the office of the possible client and the salesman had returned to the lobby, left the building, and that night had gone on to San Francisco, where he had taken a flight back to the Far East. Mason's detectives had returned to the building again and again until, finally, the missing witness had once more shown up to visit the prospective client and had been identified from the description supplied by Arthur Simmons. The salesman had not even known he was being sought until then.

Arthur Simmons was given a new trial and this jury had freed him after the salesman at last reached the witness stand. He gave Arthur Simmons an alibi by verifying his story of hearing the screams while both of them were on the elevator.

Now in the empty courtroom Mason put some papers into his briefcase. He had a real sense of satisfaction that in the case of Arthur Simmons a wrong had been righted. He was aware that in today's world, where there seemed to be so much crime, there were people who thought accused individuals received too much sympathy and aid from the law and defense attorneys like himself. He theorized that was simply because people didn't always understand that if the wrong person was convicted, then the guilty party had claimed not just one victim, but two; justice had been thwarted twice.

He picked up his briefcase. He decided that today he had made a contribution to balancing the scales of justice.

3

Perry Mason sat down in his comfortable, creaking swivel chair, swung the chair slightly around, and propped his feet on an open desk drawer.

"Now, Mrs. Adrian," he said to the woman sitting across the desk from him, "What can I do for you?"

"I believe I'm to be indicted in my husband's murder," Laurel Adrian said, biting her lip. "I would like to retain you to defend me."

Mason studied her as she spoke. She was younger than he'd thought she'd be, in her late twenties or early thirties. Her hair was coal black and cut in a short fringe and her face was quite pretty. Her figure was small-boned and slender. He thought, judging from the photographs in the news, Gilbert Adrian must have been almost twice her age. And then he remembered that she had been Adrian's second wife.

"What makes you think the police are going to indict you?"

"Because my lawyer told me so."

Mason frowned. "Then you do already have a lawyer?"

"He's the one who advised me to talk to you," Laurel said.

"Harvey Weybright: He said you might remember him. He's been my family's lawyer for years."

"Yes, I do remember Harvey. An excellent estate lawyer—"

"But not a trial lawyer," Laurel said quickly. "You see? And he said you were the best. He wants me to have you."

"Before we decide that, why don't you tell me exactly what happened, as far as you are concerned, last night. I'm aware of the accounts that have been in the news this morning. You tell me in your own words."

Laurel gazed at him steadily and related the story of what had happened from the time she arrived back at her house until the time she was taken to the station house for questioning.

"Everything I've told you I told to the police that night," she added.

"You say you reached the house before the police got there but before you went inside you discovered you'd misplaced your door keys. You were on your way back to the car to look for the keys and suddenly the police were there?"

"Yes."

"And you then returned to the car, with the police, and found your keys?"

"Yes."

"And where were the keys, exactly?"

"On the floor of the car, just inside the door. I must have dropped them accidentally when I got out of the car."

Mason was aware that Della, who was sitting a few feet away from the desk making notes of the meeting, had raised her eyebrows after she recorded the last few words he and Laurel Adrian had exchanged. He, too, wondered if she'd ever misplaced the keys before she conveniently found them again.

Mason centered his attention again on the woman across the desk. "Now let's go back a bit on what happened that evening. You said you were driving to Malibu to meet your husband, at his request. But on the way you suddenly suspected it might be a trick and you stopped and phoned the beach house and then your house, is that correct?"

"Yes. That's what happened."

"Can you recall if anyone saw you during that time? If it's

possible that anyone would remember seeing you while you were making the trip?"

"I"—she paused, frowning—"I just don't know."

"The place you made the phone call from," Mason asked, "where was that?"

"It was an outdoor phone booth. I can show you where it is, if that would help."

"Perhaps later."

Mason paused thoughtfully and said, "Turning to another matter: You and your husband were separated, I believe."

"Yes."

"And planned to divorce?"

"Yes. I imagine you know of the stories in the news of my husband's involvement with Councilwoman Janet Coleman—" She let the sentence hang in the air.

Mason nodded. "And that was the reason for your separation and impending divorce?"

"Yes."

"And were you bitter about the situation?"

"Truthfully," she said, her head raised, "I think if a marriage is not good for both parties, well, it should be ended."

Mason smiled. "That's very sensible, although usually the injured party doesn't feel that way."

"I do. And always have felt so."

"You were the second Mrs. Gilbert Adrian, I understand."

"Gil's first wife died several years before we were married," Laurel said. "They had a son, Randolph Adrian. He's now about my age. His father employed him in one of his businesses. I never saw much of him."

"There's one other aspect of your marriage we need to discuss," Mason said. "How much did you know about your husband's business affairs?"

"His business affairs?" Laurel shook her head. "Nothing, nothing at all. At least not until all those stories began to appear in the news. He never talked to me about his business."

"So you weren't aware that he might have been involved in illegal activities, as has been alleged?"

"No, I was not aware."

Mason frowned. "And therefore, I assume, he never gave you

cause to suspect that he might have made some powerful enemies?"

"No."

Laurel leaned forward suddenly, "You know, Mr. Mason, there
was a similar break-in and murder at another house on our block
about six months ago. I wonder if this could have been done by
the same person?"

"Did you mention it to the police last night?"

She nodded. "To that Lieutenant Latham. But I don't think he
was interested."

She sighed.

"All right, Mrs. Adrian," Mason said. "I think that about does it.
I'll see what I can find out from the District Attorney's office
about your possible indictment so we'll at least have some advance notice. Meanwhile, I'd like it if you would stay in close
touch with my office so we'll know where to reach you if we need
you."

He stood up and so did she.

She took his hand in both of hers and said, "This means you *will*
represent me?"

"Yes." Mason nodded. He told her what his fee would be, and
added, "I'll have an agreement prepared for you to read and sign.
Miss Street will have copies ready for you in the next day or so. Is
that satisfactory?"

"More than satisfactory," Laurel said. "I'm grateful to have
your services."

Mason nodded again.

"I plan to move out to the beach house, at least temporarily,"
Laurel Adrian said. "I don't think I want to stay another night in
that house where Gil was killed."

"Just make sure we have your phone number and address,"
Mason said.

Della showed Laurel Adrian out of the office. Mason picked up
the telephone and called his private investigator, Paul Drake, Jr.

4

Della came back into the office as Mason hung up the phone.

"Let me guess," she said. "Paul's on his way in?"

"Yep." Mason made a motion with his hand. "Sit down, Della. I want you here while I talk to Paul."

Della sat, and asked, "What do you think the chances are of getting her off?"

"Good, I'd say." Mason looked at Della quizzically. "Why else would I take the case?"

"Because you feel sorry for her. Because she's pretty. Because otherwise she'd be all alone facing the formidable array of the prosecution's forces."

"Granting that all those things are true," Mason smiled, "and I'm not admitting they are, there could be another factor."

"Which is?"

"Which is that the law says a defendant in a murder case must be proven guilty beyond a reasonable doubt."

He paused when Paul Drake, Jr., appeared at the open door, waved him in, and added, to Della, "With all the shady stuff Adrian was into there must have been half a dozen people who might have wanted him dead. If a jury can be persuaded to consider that possibility there would have to be reasonable doubt about Laurel Adrian's guilt."

"And that's going to be the premise of your defense?"

"Not necessarily. What I really want is to be able to clear her completely."

Della frowned. "Can I ask you a question, Chief?"

"What is it?"

"Well," Della said slowly, "that was a pretty fishy story she told about the keys, wasn't it? Thinking she'd lost them and then finding them so easily on the floor of the car?"

Mason smiled. "I noticed that you thought her answer was peculiar when you wrote it down."

"Well, darn it, wasn't it peculiar?"

"Yes, yes, it was," Mason said. "You're wondering if she hadn't been in the house, shot him, and was running away when the police arrived. And then that she made up the story about the keys."

"Something like that, yes."

"The police probably are wondering about the same thing. But they have no evidence to that effect. The fact is, all they have against her so far is a lot of circumstantial evidence that I'm not going to let convict her if they do indict her."

Della nodded her head. "You're right, Chief."

Mason turned his attention to Drake, who was seated in the big leather client's chair in front of the desk. "What did you find out, Paul?"

Drake said, "As you asked on the phone, I made calls to a couple of my sources to find out who's in charge of the Adrian case in the District Attorney's office. Would it surprise you to learn that it's the D.A. himself?"

Mason ran a thumb down the side of his chin. "Carter Phillips in person, well, well, well. No, Paul, it doesn't surprise me. What it tells me is the political establishment in this city and state want the top legal gun in to try for a quick conviction."

"Otherwise," Drake suggested, "the voters might begin to speculate that Adrian was really shut up to prevent him from going to trial. And maybe spilling the beans on who he bribed?"

"Exactly." Mason nodded. "And how convenient it will be for

them if Adrian's wife is convicted of his murder. All those alleged scandalous charges of political corruption will be buried in the grave with him."

"Why, that would be just terrible," Della said sympathetically, "if she's innocent."

"Which is what we're going to try to find out and prove, starting now," Mason said. "Paul, I want you to uncover everything you can about Gil Adrian's background. And I don't care how many men you have to put on the job."

"No problem."

"And, Paul, everything includes checking out those rumors about his ties to the mob here and in Las Vegas. And his involvement with Councilwoman Janet Coleman. Also, he had a son, Randolph Adrian, from his first marriage. He works for one of the Adrian companies. Let's find out what we can about him."

Mason swung around in his chair. "Della, I want you to go to the library and get me copies of all the stories that have appeared about Gil Adrian."

He stood up. "As for me, I'm on my way to visit my favorite lieutenant in Homicide. Let's see what I can pry out of him about the case they're trying to build against our client."

5

Lieutenant Ray Dallas glanced up from the report he was reading as Perry Mason entered the office at Police Headquarters.

"Hello, Counselor. I hear you had quite a victory in court this morning."

Mason smiled. "You could say it went the way I wanted."

The two men shook hands. Ray Dallas was of medium height, stocky in build, his hair more-pepper-than-salt gray. He had a strong, still-youthful face and his eyes were bright, alert, watchful, whatever they focused upon. He had worked hard to earn the same respect held by the man he'd replaced on the Homicide Squad, Lieutenant Tragg. And he had succeeded.

Perry Mason and Tragg, although often separated by philosophical prosecution/defense approaches to criminal cases, had been good friends before Tragg retired. Now, in a similar manner, Mason and Dallas were good friends.

Lieutenant Dallas sat back in his chair, arms crossed behind his head.

"So, what brings you in here to see me when I would have thought you'd be out somewhere celebrating?"

"The Gilbert Adrian murder."

Dallas uncrossed his arms. "And your interest is?"

"The wife. I'm representing her," Mason said.

Dallas gave a soft chuckle. "You really pick some beauts for clients, Counselor."

"I don't pick them," Mason said gruffly. "They pick me."

"It comes out to the same thing." Dallas shook his head in mock concern. "Cases that are the toughest nuts for you to crack."

Mason shrugged and said nothing.

Still shaking his head, Dallas asked, "What is it you want from me?"

"Mrs. Adrian told me that you conducted the interrogation when she was taken to the local station house last night after her husband's murder was discovered," Mason said.

"I questioned her, yes."

"A Lieutenant Latham, I believe, was originally in charge of the case. I assume, therefore, you were ordered to step in and take over the investigation."

Dallas waved a hand in the air. "Nothing unusual about that. Word came down that the commissioner wanted the investigation run out of Headquarters. That's what we're here for."

"And the fact that Gilbert Adrian was who he was has nothing to do with it?" Mason asked.

"For your information, Counselor, there was another homicide in that same area a few months back. The local precinct police, including Lieutenant Latham, were never able to solve it. Why wouldn't it sound logical to you that this time the commissioner would want his senior men to take charge?"

"It still doesn't sound to me like the kind of homicide calling for the services of Headquarters experts."

Mason paused as if he had finished his statement. Then he added, "Nor, I might further suggest, the services of Carter Phillips personally to prosecute."

"If I read you right," Lieutenant Dallas said in a noncommittal tone, "you're implying orders are coming down from somewhere high up to ensure the wife takes the fall for the murder. And ends all the political scandal that was swirling around Adrian."

"The thought did cross my mind."

"Mine, too." Dallas shrugged. "But, on the other hand, am I

supposed to ignore all the evidence pointing to her guilt? She had motive; he was dumping her for another woman. She had opportunity; she was at the scene of the murder. She had the means; the thirty-eight revolver lying on the desk. If you ask me, it's a pretty strong case against her."

"Sure," Mason said, "as far as circumstantial evidence is concerned."

"There's collaborative evidence, as well," Dallas said.

"I'd sure like to hear it." Mason waited expectantly, not at all certain the lieutenant would tell him more.

Dallas frowned thoughtfully before he spoke. "I can't see any harm in sharing certain facts with you since you're going to hear them soon enough, when the indictment is handed down." He pushed his chair back from the desk. "I want to show you some photographs of the scene, Adrian's den, at the time he was shot."

Dallas went to a file cabinet, took out a folder, and came back and sat in his chair.

"The D.A. has copies of these prints. And I went to the house last night and saw the scene for myself after I finished the interrogation of the wife at the station house."

He kept talking as he took the photographs from the folder and spread them out on the desk top for Mason's inspection.

"Adrian's den was a shambles. Papers, ledgers, letters, receipts, scattered everywhere. Scraps of torn paper filled the wastebaskets; there was warm ash from other papers that had been burned in the den fireplace. And the wall safe was open and empty."

Mason studied the photographs in silence. There were shots of the desk with papers strewn about, shots of a couple of wastebaskets filled with strips of paper, shots of a pile of white ash in the fireplace, a shot of the empty interior of the wall safe.

Mason finally looked up but said nothing.

Dallas said, "You do understand the implications of all this for your client? There's simply no way Adrian himself could have created such a mess."

"Why's that?"

"Because of the time element." Dallas opened a desk drawer and took out a sheet of paper. "We've verified, with witnesses, Adrian's whereabouts, and from when to when, throughout the entire day yesterday before he was killed."

He read from the paper. "He was in his office from nine A.M. yesterday until five in the afternoon. He even ate lunch at his desk. From five-fifteen to eight-thirty P.M. he was with his accountant preparing for his court appearance today. At nine o'clock last night he walked into the Oaks Restaurant, a half-hour drive from his lawyer's office. He was at the restaurant until nine-forty-five, the approximate time he shot and killed the man who had joined him in the restaurant. And, finally, less than thirty minutes later, the police found him dead at his desk in the den of his house."

Dallas returned the paper to his desk drawer. "We've clocked the driving time from the restaurant to the house. Even at high speed it's a minimum of ten minutes. Which makes it just about impossible for him to have emptied the safe and most of the desk and torn up and burned papers and records. And to have been shot, I might add."

Mason nodded agreeably. "So, I gather, you think someone else must have ransacked the den."

"Specifically, we think your client did. And he walked in on her. He had the gun with him he'd just used. She, the wife, somehow got hold of the gun and shot him."

"Were there any prints on the gun?"

"It was wiped clean."

"Why couldn't it have been someone else ransacking the den who shot him?" Mason asked.

"Because there were no signs of forced entry at the house. We have no reason to believe anyone else was there. *And* your client *was* there when the police arrived. In addition, she has no witnesses who can place her anywhere else at any time that evening. There just doesn't seem to be any explanation other than that she shot him."

"Since I believe she's innocent," Mason said, "I'll have to find another explanation."

He paused for a moment and asked, "What about the fellow Adrian shot at the restaurant? As I recall from news accounts at the time, the police didn't know his identity."

"We still don't. All that was found on him was some cash in his pants pocket, a phony driver's license he'd used to rent the car he drove to the restaurant, and the car keys. There was also a loaded twenty-two-caliber pistol in the holster strapped to his ankle."

"A twenty-two? The weapon of choice for hit men, I believe."

"In frequent cases, yes."

"That would mean someone other than my client wanted Adrian dead."

"Even if that's true," Dallas said, "one thing's for sure, *he* didn't kill Adrian."

"And neither did my client," Mason said firmly.

"I might be more inclined to agree with you, Counselor," Dallas said softly, "if there wasn't also the matter of the polygraph test."

"What polygraph test?" Mason was astonished.

"You didn't know about it?"

"I did not."

"Well, she did take a polygraph test." Dallas nodded. "She agreed to it, seemed eager to take it, in fact. We did it all by the book. She was told we couldn't use the results in court and that she didn't have to take it if she didn't want to. Her lawyer, Weybright, was present. He tried to talk her out of it but she wouldn't listen to him."

"Just as well she has a new lawyer now," Mason said irritably.

Dallas smiled slightly. "At any rate, she took the test and flunked it."

"You still don't have enough to indict her."

"I might point out to you," Dallas said quietly, "it's still an ongoing investigation."

Mason said abruptly, "I think I'd like to take a look at the scene of the crime."

"Want some company?" Dallas asked.

"Let's go," Mason said.

6

"The forensic guys are still doing some wrap-up work in here,"
Lieutenant Dallas said to Mason as they entered the room where
Gilbert Adrian had been killed.

They had been admitted to the house by a uniformed policeman posted at the front door. Another policeman stood at the
door to the den. In answer to Mason's question, that policeman
had informed him that Laurel Adrian was upstairs packing her
clothes for a move to the Adrian beach house. Mason had asked
that Laurel not leave until he had had a chance to speak with her.
The policeman said he would see that she received the message.

The two men from the forensic team, working in shirt sleeves,
looked up without much interest at Mason and Dallas, nodded to
the lieutenant, and went on with their search through the papers
and folders that littered the desk and floor. Now and then they
dusted for latent fingerprints.

"Everything's pretty much the way it was last night," Dallas
said. "Except of course the body's gone."

Mason looked at the armchair which still lay overturned behind
the desk. A chalk outline had been drawn on the floor beside the
desk to indicate exactly where the body had rested.

"Where was the gun found?" Mason asked. "The thirty-eight?"

Dallas pointed to a spot on the desk top directly in front of where the armchair would have sat if it had been upright.

"Here, on top of that pile of papers," Dallas said.

"The barrel pointed how?"

"Straight toward where Adrian would have been sitting in the chair. Then there must have been a scuffle and the chair went over backward."

The lieutenant moved around behind the desk and chair and indicated two holes in the wall behind the desk. "Two bullets were dug out of the wall. They must have been the first couple of shots that went wild before the shooter hit the target. Ballistics has the bullets."

"How many cartridges were still in the gun when it was found?" Mason asked.

"The gun was empty," Dallas said. "Which would figure. Adrian shot the guy at the Oaks Restaurant and then came here without reloading. He walked in and discovered somebody had been here going through his desk and files and safe. He must have laid the gun on the desk while he sat in the chair trying to figure out what was missing. Then, whoever was here came out of hiding, picked up the gun, and fired at him. The first couple of shots missed. Adrian was probably trying to get around the desk when the killer shot him twice."

"It could have been that way." Mason nodded. "But that's no evidence that implicates Laurel Adrian. Anyone could have shot him."

Dallas jerked a thumb at the two men dusting for fingerprints. "We're still gathering evidence, don't forget."

Mason shrugged.

Laurel appeared in the doorway. She had a small suitcase in her hand.

"You wanted to see me, Mr. Mason?"

Mason said to Dallas, "I'd like to have a few minutes alone in here with my client."

"Yeah, okay. Just see to it that neither she nor you touch anything." Dallas made a motion to the two men from the forensic team. The three of them left the room.

Laurel came into the room and put her suitcase down. The

policeman at the door remained so he could watch Mason and Laurel although he could not hear what they said.

"I want you to take a careful look around," Mason instructed Laurel. "See if you notice anything in the room that you might have missed last night. The lieutenant assures me the room looks about the way it did then."

It was apparent to Mason that Laurel found being in the room distasteful. But she looked carefully at the desk, the open safe, the ashes in the fireplace. He noticed she avoided looking at the chalk outline on the floor where Adrian's body had been found.

"What are those?" she asked, pointing to the holes in the wall behind the desk.

"Bullet holes, Dallas said. He says they dug the bullets out and ballistics has them. He thinks whoever killed your husband missed with the first two shots."

"Oh."

Mason had followed her around behind the desk. She pointed to an open desk drawer, the middle drawer on the right-hand side of the desk.

"That's where they found my gun," she said. "It's so funny. I had forgotten it was there until they showed me."

Mason glanced at the open wall safe. "Laurel, did you know the combination to the safe?"

She shook her head again. "Gil never told me and I never asked."

"I understand the door to the safe was open."

"Yes."

Mason glanced sideways at her. "Did anyone else have a key to the house? Was there any way anyone else could have entered the house without breaking in?"

"No, not that I know of," she said. "I just imagined that Gil opened the door and let in whoever it was that shot him."

"It couldn't have been that way. There just wasn't time for everything that happened to happen."

"How long would it have taken for someone to appear at the house, to be let in by Gil, and to have shot him and left?" she asked. "I would think only a matter of minutes. Why wouldn't that be enough time?"

"Enough time to shoot him, yes," Mason agreed. "But there

wasn't enough time for your husband to have emptied the safe and most of the desk and to have destroyed papers and records in the period between leaving the restaurant and being found dead by you and the police."

"But he could have done most of that before he went to the restaurant."

Mason shook his head. "The police have an exact record of your husband's whereabouts for the entire day yesterday right up to the moment he left the restaurant, and they found him shortly afterward at the house, dead."

"But if Gil didn't open the safe and clear out the desk and all that, who did?" Laurel asked.

Mason didn't answer, and after a moment's silence, Laurel said quietly, "I see. I'm beginning to understand what the police suspect happened. They think I was the one who was at the house, going through the safe and the desk, and that Gil walked in on me. That's it, isn't it?"

"Yes. That's what the police suspect happened."

"Well, it's not true." Her voice was firm. "I wasn't at the house earlier, I didn't kill him, and I don't know who else was there or who killed him."

"All right," Mason said, "we'll just have to find out the answer."

He looked at her quizzically. "There is one other matter. Lieutenant Dallas told me you took a polygraph test; I don't remember your mentioning it to me."

"I didn't think it was important. I took it because I thought it would clear me."

"What questions did they ask you?"

"Did I kill my husband? I didn't. I said no."

"What else?"

She waved a hand in the air. "They repeated all the questions they'd asked me earlier at the house and I answered them. And they asked me if I knew who might have killed him. They said they couldn't use my answers in court. That's true, isn't it?"

"Yes."

"Well, then, you see? I had hoped by taking the test, I could end all their questioning of me."

Mason decided not to discuss with her the fact that she had failed the polygraph test. Instead he said, "In the future, Laurel, I want you to tell me everything. I'll decide what's important and what's not."

She nodded.

"I'm glad we understand that." He added, "You may go on along to the beach house now."

She looked grateful to be leaving the room as she picked up her suitcase and went out.

Mason was standing at the window looking out when Dallas and the other two men returned to the den.

"Do you have any new information for me, Counselor?" Dallas asked.

Mason was watching Laurel as she got into her car and backed out of the driveway.

At the end of the drive she turned and drove away. Just as he started to leave the window he spotted a car parked down the street start up and follow Laurel.

"Do you have surveillance on my client?" he asked Dallas, suspecting that was the case.

"No," Dallas said. "There was no such order."

"Well, somebody's following her," Mason said, moving fast toward the door.

He had left his car parked in front of the Adrian house. As he sped down the winding hill road leading to the Santa Monica Freeway below, he was afraid he'd lost Laurel's car and the car following her. When he rounded a final curve, he spotted both cars, Laurel's car in front, stopped at the intersection.

He was close enough behind the other car to read the license plate. He could see that the driver, the sole occupant of the car, was a man.

Mason reached for his car phone, called Della at the office, and read off the license numbers. "Get Paul to check the Motor Vehicle Bureau. I want to know who owns that car."

Up ahead, both cars turned on to the freeway and sped away. Mason lost sight of them in the rush of traffic.

7

Paul Drake, Jr., gave a low, sharp whistle when Perry Mason finished bringing him up to date on the latest developments involving Laurel Adrian.

Mason put his hand up to cover a sudden smile, knowing Drake would never understand the reason for the smile. It was because Mason had experienced a moment of fond recollection when he heard the sharp whistle; the reaction of Paul Drake, Jr., had been so like the reaction on past occasions of Paul Drake, Sr., who had done private investigating work for Mason for many years.

When the elder Drake had retired, Paul Drake, Jr., had taken over the detective agency founded by his father and had continued to work closely with Perry Mason. Frequently, in the time since then, the lawyer had been struck by the small similarities in mannerisms between the father and the son.

Drake said, "Perry, from the way you describe the scene in Adrian's den, can you be *sure* he didn't return to the house that night, find Laurel going through his safe and papers, and then she killed him?"

"Of course I can't be sure," Mason said. "But neither can the prosecution. And that's what they have to prove. And beyond a reasonable doubt."

"Well, according to that license plate you asked me to check out with the Motor Vehicle Bureau, the cops are keeping a close eye on her."

"You mean that was an unmarked police car tailing her?"

"So says the Motor Vehicle Bureau." Drake nodded. "The car's licensed to the local precinct in the neighborhood of the Adrian house."

Mason frowned. "Ray Dallas told me there was no police surveillance on her." He snapped his fingers. "I have a hunch Dallas himself doesn't know about it."

"You mean the local precinct is carrying on its own secret investigation of her."

"Something like that. The original officer on the murder scene was a Lieutenant Frank Latham. He was relieved of the investigation and replaced by Dallas, from Headquarters."

"And now this Latham would like to solve the case on his own?" Drake suggested.

"Just maybe." Mason nodded. "Especially since about six months ago there was a similar robbery and murder in the same neighborhood and the local precinct hasn't been able to solve it. Which reminds me, Paul, get one of your men to look into that earlier case. Let's see if there's any possible connection between the two."

"Makes sense." Drake pulled a notebook from his pocket. "I've been digging into Gil Adrian's background, and I've also assigned several of my best operatives to the case." He looked up.

"Okay, let's hear what you have."

"To begin with, Perry, Gil Adrian *was* wired into a lot of unsavory stuff, all right. There seems to be no question but that he bribed politicians to get better deals for himself and his associates, that he did business with at least one alleged mob figure in Vegas, and that he had a hot and heavy romance going with Councilwoman Janet Coleman. One of my men has a buddy who was an investigator for the federal prosecutor on the case they were going to bring to trial against Adrian. My operative thinks his buddy will supply us with some leaks, off the record."

"A good beginning, Paul," Mason said. "What about the son, Randolph?"

Drake said, "He works in the main office of Adrian Enterprises, as the overall holding company is called. I didn't try to see him. My information is that he was dominated by his father and has never done much on his own."

Drake passed over a piece of paper. "This is his phone number and address."

"I'll certainly want to talk to him. And to Janet Coleman, as well."

Mason tucked the paper into a corner of his desk blotter. "Paul, I'd like to find out more about this mob figure in Las Vegas. If the unidentified man Adrian shot, the night he himself was killed, was a hit man, the connection would probably be there."

"Sounds likely." Drake nodded. "All I know so far is that the Vegas guy's name is Anselmo Costa. He's a newcomer from back east. What I hear is that Adrian was a partner in a new hotel-casino in Las Vegas, The Palms Palace, and the unverified rumor is that Costa was a silent partner. One of my operatives has a friend who's a blackjack dealer there. What do you think, Perry?"

"I think," Mason said, "you should try your luck at The Palms Palace in Las Vegas."

Drake grinned. "My sentiments exactly." He started to rise from his chair.

Mason held up a hand. "One thing, though, Paul. I don't want you to go alone. Take along your man who knows the blackjack dealer."

"Agreed."

Della Street tapped on the door, opened it and, seeing Drake, said, "Hi, Paul." She looked at Mason. "I'm sorry, Chief. I thought you were alone. Am I intruding?"

"It's all right, Della. Come on in. Paul and I just finished our business."

Della had an armful of newspaper clippings which she placed on the desk. "Here are some more stories on Gilbert Adrian to add to the ones I collected yesterday. I can almost guarantee this is the complete file."

Mason glanced down at the top page of the clippings where there was a photograph of Gil Adrian in his Stetson hat, aviator glasses, and beard. Above the photograph was a headline: LEADING BUSINESSMAN MURDERED.

Mason shook his head. "The words and picture say it all about the facade Mr. Gilbert Adrian hid behind."

"Speaking of words and pictures," Della said, "take a look at the front page of the latest edition of today's paper."

She held the newspaper up.

There was a photograph of Laurel Adrian on one side of the page under the headline WIFE QUIZZED IN ADRIAN MURDER.

On the other side of the page was a photograph of Perry Mason and, above it, the headline FAMOUS LAWYER RETAINED BY MRS. ADRIAN.

"I don't know whether that looks like the face of a murderess," Drake joked, "but the other photo looks like the face of a famous lawyer, all right."

Mason smiled and said good-naturedly, "On your way, Paul."

Drake grinned, gave a wave of his hand, and headed toward the door.

The intercom on the desk buzzed. Mason flipped the switch. "Yes, Gertie?"

The voice of Gertie, the receptionist in the outer office, came back over the intercom in a whisper: "Mr. Mason, there's a gentleman out here who demands to see you. A Mr. Randolph Adrian."

Mason looked at Della Street and raised his eyebrows. He told Gertie: "Tell Mr. Adrian I'll see him in just a moment."

Mason made a motion to Della. "Show him in, Della."

Della left the office. Mason quickly cleaned off his desk. The newspaper and Drake's note with Randolph Adrian's address and phone number were all out of sight before Della returned and introduced Randolph Adrian.

The younger Adrian was as tall as his father had been but much thinner. His hair was reddish and so was the color of his face as he stood and shook hands with Mason across the desk.

Randolph Adrian waited until Della had withdrawn from the office, closing the door behind her, before he slammed a copy of the newspaper down on the desk in obvious anger.

"Mr. Mason, I can't believe a man of your reputation is going to defend *her*!" He stabbed a finger at the photograph of Laurel Adrian on the newspaper page.

"Mr. Adrian," Mason said quietly, "Laurel Adrian hasn't been charged with anything. I'm simply her attorney. Why don't you have a seat and tell me exactly what's on your mind."

Adrian sat down on the edge of the client's chair. "She murdered my father. It's only a matter of time before she's charged. And you're going to try to get her off."

"Now, hold on a minute! You can't know that she killed your father. Not unless you were present at the time and saw it happen. I presume you are not prepared to state that such was the case?"

"Of course I'm not," Adrian sputtered.

"Then you can't know," Mason said reasonably. "That will be up to a judge and jury to determine."

"And they will, when all the facts are known. And, at that time, too, you may be sorry you undertook her defense."

Mason sat back in his chair. "Mr. Adrian, if you possess any information to prove your stepmother killed your father, I would be eager to hear it."

Adrian said, "She only married him for his money and then she killed him for it."

"You said 'when all the facts are known'; not just a supposition on your part?"

"What my father planned to do about his will is certainly a fact. They were divorcing, remember? He made arrangements to change his will, cutting her out of it. And the day before it's to be done, he's killed. That's a fact!"

Mason hid his surprise at this new piece of information. "But that's not proof."

"It's all the proof I need. What's more, it should be interesting to see what the judge and jury think after they hear about it."

Mason waited and, when Adrian appeared to have nothing more to add, asked, "Is there anything else you'd like to tell me, Mr. Adrian?"

"I should think that would be enough."

Randolph Adrian stood.

Mason pressed the buzzer under his desk and Della, opening the door, appeared almost instantly.

"Della, would you show Mr. Adrian out, please."

Mason swung around in his chair and stared out the window thoughtfully. At every turn, it seemed, the noose of incriminating circumstances was being tightened around the neck of his client. Not that he would believe any accusations leveled by Randolph Adrian. But the prosecution would, eagerly.

"What did he want?" Della asked, returning to the office.

Mason turned back in his chair. "You can be sure it was nothing favorable to his stepmother. He says his father was planning to change his will, cutting Laurel off, and, a day before, was killed. The whole world is out to convict her. You can count on it."

"Well, I think, with your help, she's just spunky enough to beat the charge."

"Or perhaps," Mason's words were musing, "just audacious."

"What does that mean?"

"The way a jury might see her; if she was audacious enough to shoot her husband she's audacious enough to make a good witness for herself."

Della shook her head. "You know, Perry, sometimes I don't understand you at all. I know you feel about her the way I do, yet you talk as if you're not completely convinced."

Mason grinned. "I have this lifelong habit of trying to view people and what they do and say from various angles, frequently from angles of vision different from my own. It's a habit that's stood me in good stead."

"Oh, you! Sometimes I think you just say things to get me riled up."

"There's always that possibility." He was still grinning. He glanced at his watch and saw that the time was a few minutes before 6 P.M.

He stood abruptly and started toward the door. "Lock up, will you please, Della? There's someone I want to see and I think I know the place to find him."

Downstairs, outside his office building, he grabbed a taxicab. "Clay's Bar and Grill," he said, pulling some bills from his pocket.

The restaurant was a popular drinking and dining place for the city's lawyers and law enforcement officials, particularly at the end of the day around the cocktail hour, as it was now.

As soon as he entered the bar, crowded as it was, Mason quickly spotted David Niles, the man he was seeking, standing alone, a drink in his hand, on the far side of the room.

The federal prosecutor had an appearance that stood out in any crowd. He was tall and erect in bearing, his prematurely graying hair was carefully barbered, and his dark blue suit custom-tailored.

Mason had known David Niles over the years since Niles had been a young lawyer on the staff of the governor in Sacramento, then as an assistant state prosecutor, and after he had risen to his present prominence.

"Perry!" Niles greeted Mason with warmth, shaking hands.

"David, you're looking well."

"You, too," Niles said.

Mason ordered a drink.

The federal prosecutor said musingly, "I have a feeling this encounter, pleasant as it is, didn't come about exactly by coincidence."

"True." Mason nodded his head. "I thought perhaps we should have a little chat."

"Why not?"

They carried their drinks to a table in a corner of the room out of listening range of the drinkers standing around the bar.

"So, you're going to defend the Adrian widow?" Niles said, coming directly to the point.

Mason said, "And it occurred to me that in the course of that defense I might be of help to you and you of help to me."

"Let's discuss the first part of your proposition first," Niles said, smiling slightly.

Mason said, "Let's say I plan to put as much heat as I can on Anselmo Costa. Interest you?"

"Possibly."

"It's my guess, now that Gilbert Adrian has been eliminated, you may have a problem tying Costa in to your corruption probe."

"Possibly," Niles said again, cautiously.

"Knowing you, I'd say you'd be plenty sore."

"Maybe I am. So how are you going to help me?"

"If I have to go to court to defend Laurel Adrian, I'll get a chance at Costa that you can't get."

"What makes you think you can involve Anselmo Costa as part of your defense of your client?"

Mason said, "If the D.A. indicts her, he's going to have to bring into the case the matter of the man Adrian shot at the Oaks Restaurant. One way or another that gives me an opportunity to tie that man in to Costa."

"Suppose you can? What good is that going to do me with my corruption probe?"

"At the very least," Mason said, "I'll have pulled Costa into the clutches of the legal system. Then—who knows?—maybe he'll trip up, or find he'll have to try to make some kind of deal, which could give you a crack at him. In exchange, you can be of help to me."

"Anything I'd be able to give you," Niles said slowly, "you'd have to use indirectly. The corruption probe is still ongoing."

"I understand." Mason nodded. "What I need from you now would never have to enter into the record of my defense."

"Ask me what you want me to tell you and I'll decide."

Mason leaned forward. "Did you really have Adrian nailed on the charges you brought against him?"

"Absolutely. There was no way for him to wiggle out."

Mason grinned. "Then it's my hunch he made a plea-bargain deal with you."

Niles nodded his head in agreement.

"You expected him to spill the whole can of beans, right?"

"That was the deal."

"Well! Well! Well!" Mason sat back, a satisfied look on his face. "And then somebody comes along and shoots him dead and shuts him up permanently. Everybody he might have named breathes easier. It seems to me it would have to have been a hell of a coincidence for his wife to pick this particular time to kill him."

"You're trying to convince the wrong prosecutor," Niles said, smiling. "Tell it to Carter Phillips."

"Off the record," Mason said, "don't you believe, as I do, that the man Adrian shot at the Oaks Restaurant was a hit man sent to silence him?"

"Off the record." Niles nodded. "But believing it and proving it are two different things and, besides, the man at the restaurant didn't kill Adrian. If he had, you can be sure I'd be going after him, *and* whoever hired him, with all the resource of the federal government.

"I saw the scene at the Adrian house." Mason frowned. "It appeared to me that maybe what was going on there was that Adrian was making preparations to skip the country and renege on his deal with you."

"The thought occurred to me, after the fact," Niles conceded.

"Did the thought also occur to you that there might have been a second hit man who succeeded where the first one failed?"

"I'd sure like some proof. We haven't been able to turn up any. And neither has the L.A.P.D."

"Maybe I can," Mason said. He finished off his drink. "You'll notice I didn't ask you off the record if you believed Laurel Adrian is guilty."

Niles grinned. "With you as her lawyer, I'm going to withhold judgment until all the evidence is in."

8

"Paul, are you all right?"

There was concern in Perry Mason's voice as he waited outside the barred cell of the jail in Las Vegas until the guard opened the door. Mason went inside.

Paul Drake, Jr., looked up from where he was sitting on the bunk bed.

"Thanks for coming so promptly, Perry."

Drake's face was bruised and swollen, his left eye was black and half closed. One sleeve of his jacket had been ripped away at the shoulder and there was a tear at the knee of his right pants leg. His clothes were shapeless and sodden and smelled of alcohol.

"I chartered a plane in L.A. as soon as I could after your investigator, Joe Lennart, phoned me," Mason said.

"Is Joe okay?"

Mason nodded. He pulled a stool over and sat in front of Drake. The guard had disappeared. Outside, it was early dawn.

"Now tell me what happened," Mason said.

Drake's lips were puffy and he had some difficulty in talking.

"I followed your instructions and brought Joe Lennart with me from Los Angeles. We got into Vegas late yesterday afternoon. Lennart had arranged for us to meet with the blackjack dealer he knows who works at The Palms Palace casino. Incidentally, Perry, the dealer's a young woman, a fact Joe neglected to mention to me. Not that it matters."

Drake paused and touched a hand gently to the side of his face, wincing.

Mason said, "Take your time."

Drake said, "We met her at a small bar off the Strip. Melanie Sandford's her name. I had a copy of a photograph of the man Adrian shot. The police had taken the picture of him after he was dead, of course. I managed to get a copy through a friend in the L.A.P.D. I showed it to her and she recognized him. She didn't know his name but she said she knew him by sight."

"From the casino?"

Drake nodded. "And not only that. She said most of the time that he was at The Palms Palace, he was in the company of Anselmo Costa. As well as we could work out the time frame, he was in Las Vegas for about ten days or two weeks and then was gone shortly before he turned up dead in L.A., if her identification of him is accurate."

"That would tie him, through Costa and The Palms Palace hotel-casino, to Gil Adrian," Mason said.

"Exactly," Drake agreed. "So, last night, after we talked to Melanie, Joe and I went to The Palms Palace casino. We separated before we went in so nobody would connect us up and so we could keep an eye on one another. Toward midnight, in between working the blackjack tables, Melanie managed to point out Anselmo Costa to me when he came into the casino to shoot craps. I waited my chance and then when he left the craps table, I identified myself, showed him the photograph, and asked if he knew who the man was."

Drake paused again and shook his head. "Within seconds of the time I approached him, I was surrounded by a squad of goons who suddenly appeared out of nowhere. Costa held them back long enough to hiss at me that I was trying to shake him down, showing him a picture of a man who was obviously dead and asking if he knew the man. He turned away, snapped his fingers, and the squad of goons bounced me out of the casino."

"And they beat you up like this?" Mason asked indignantly.

"Oh, no," Drake said quickly. "Costa's too smart for that. He told them to see that I was safely escorted from the premises. And I was."

"Then?" Mason made a questioning motion.

Drake said, "Once I was outside, I figured I'd head back to the car Joe and I had rented and wait for Joe there. I realized he couldn't come running out of the casino right behind me."

"And on the way to the car you were waylaid and beaten."

"That's the way it happened," Drake said. "We'd left the car about a block away. I never saw the guys who grabbed me. I think there were only two. They were there behind me before I even realized. They pulled me into an alleyway and one held me from behind while the other one worked me over. I never had a chance. When I went down, just before I lost consciousness, I was aware that what seemed like a gallon of liquor was being poured over me. And I remember hearing a gunshot. I think I thought I was finished."

Mason rubbed his chin. "And of course that's the way the police found you."

"Yes. After the police brought me in they told me they'd received an anonymous phone call reporting a gunshot and a man lying in an alley. They responded and found me. There was a gun there, too, with one bullet fired from it. They said they were holding me for investigation. My investigator, Joe Lennart, finally located me here. I told him to phone you."

Mason stood. "You did the right thing, Paul, in having me called. I've already spoken to a judge. He's working now to get you out of here and it shouldn't take long. Meanwhile, I'm staying here with you."

Drake looked relieved even though he said, "You don't have to stay here with me, Perry."

"I'm staying," Mason said firmly. "And while we're waiting, Joe Lennart's getting us hotel rooms. Not at The Palms Palace, I might add. Also, he's going to pick up his friend, the blackjack dealer. He thought his friend might be in some danger and I agreed, even though I didn't know it was a young woman. They'll be waiting for us."

"I think maybe we should all get out of town," Drake said.

Mason said, "We will. But first we're going to get you patched up, cleaned up, and into some new clothes. And I'm going to have a serious conversation with Mr. Anselmo Costa. Then we'll get out of town."

9

"Mr. Perry Mason! Please come in. I'm Graham Kendrick, Mr. Costa's attorney. Mr. Costa's on a long-distance phone call in the other room. He'll be in shortly. Would you like some refreshment? Something to drink, perhaps, while we're waiting?"

"No, no, thank you."

Kendrick had started toward the bar on the far side of the room after shaking hands with Mason.

"Then I think I'll have a Perrier," Kendrick said.

He was in his early fifties, a man of medium height, and several pounds too heavy for that height. His hair was gray, his face florid, and the light from outside reflected off the gold frames of his glasses.

Mason looked around the room, the living room, of the penthouse atop The Palms Palace Hotel. The furnishings looked to be custom-made and covered in costly fabrics. The room was circular with windows curving around all sides, the drapes pulled open to reveal a view in all directions of mountains and desert surrounding the city of Las Vegas.

Kendrick came back with a glass in his hand. "I want you to

know it's a real pleasure to meet you, Mr. Mason. As you are no doubt accustomed to hearing, your reputation has preceded you."

"That's kind of you to say."

Mason smiled briefly and turned as he heard a voice behind him, "Ah, Mr. Mason. Anselmo Costa here."

Costa was under six feet in height, thin, middle-aged, dark-haired and dressed in a dark suit with a flower in his coat lapel.

"Have a seat," Costa said. "I believe you told me on the phone that you had a matter of importance to discuss with me."

"I have," Mason said. "I'm representing Mrs. Gilbert Adrian, who is charged with the murder of her husband. I believe you were acquainted with Mr. Adrian?"

"I did know Mr. Adrian, yes." Costa nodded. "He and I both were frequent guests at the hotel and casino. We met on occasion."

"I was given to understand that he had a financial interest in The Palms Palace."

"Mr. Mason"—Costa leaned forward earnestly—"I simply wouldn't know about that. I myself am not financially involved in The Palms Palace. You do understand that, don't you?"

"I had been led to believe otherwise." Mason made a gesture around the room. "And all this?"

Costa laughed easily. "I rent these quarters several times a year when I come out from Chicago to relax. I'm afraid your information is incorrect. If you want to inquire about Mr. Adrian's participation, if any, in the hotel, I suggest you talk to the owners of record."

"I see." Mason frowned. "Then perhaps you will be patient enough to assist me on another matter."

Mason took from his coat pocket the picture of the man Adrian had shot.

Costa looked at the photograph. "I think I was shown this just last night. A man approached me in the casino downstairs with this picture."

"The man who approached you works for me. He's a private detective in my employ."

"His purpose in showing me the photograph was not made clear to me," Costa said.

"Perhaps he never had time to tell you what he wanted," Mason said. "I believe he was rather forcibly hustled out of the casino as soon as he tried to speak to you."

Costa smiled thinly. "The security people do have a tendency to step in when they anticipate trouble. They do not like it when any of their preferred customers, and I happen to be one of them, is annoyed. I'm sure it was simply an unfortunate incident."

"That may very well be the case." Mason nodded. "However, a more unfortunate incident occurred after he was put out of the casino. A few minutes later, while walking to his car, he was ambushed and beaten and wound up in jail."

"How terrible!" Costa said. He handed the photograph back to Mason. "And, tell me, Mr. Mason, what is your interest in the picture of this man?"

Mason said bluntly. "I want to know if you knew him?"

"Yes."

"He's the man Gil Adrian shot and killed the night Adrian himself was killed."

"Ah-ha!" Costa said. "Now I see! As I recall, the police did not know the identity of this man. And of course I never saw a photograph of him before. Now, it is all made clear to me."

"You did know him, then?" Mason asked.

"From the casino," Costa said. "He was always around for a while. I can't say I knew him, actually."

"But you knew his name?"

Costa stood up. "Why don't you come with me, Mr. Mason?" Costa waved a hand at the lawyer, Graham Kendrick, to accompany them.

They went out of the penthouse suite and rode the elevator to the lobby. Costa went to the desk, Mason and Kendrick following, and asked for the hotel manager.

When the manager appeared, Costa introduced Mason and added, "Please show him the photograph."

Mason produced the picture. Costa said to the manager, "Mr. Mason is interested in learning the identity of the person in the photograph. You remember him? He was a guest here at the hotel a while back."

The manager turned and lifted down a register ledger; he

riffled through the pages and then stopped. He swung the ledger around to the front of the desk so Mason could read it.

The manager poked a finger at an entry written there: Karl Braundorff, 921 East 2nd Street, New York City, and said, "He was here from May first to May ninth."

Mason made a note of the name and address.

"Well, there you have it, Mr. Mason." Costa shook hands, nodded, and walked away. His lawyer followed him.

Earlier, Mason had put Paul Drake, Jr., Joe Lennart, and Melanie Sandford on a plane back to L.A. Now he started out of The Palms Palace hotel. There were slot machines set up everywhere around the lobby. Mason paused in front of one of the slot machines near the entrance, took a quarter from his pocket, dropped it into the slot and pulled the handle. The cylinders whirred and two lemons and what looked to him like a raspberry came up, a combination that didn't pay off.

It was, Mason thought wryly, a combination similar to what he'd gotten out of the meeting at the hotel earlier: two lemons, Costa and Kendrick, and a raspberry, the runaround they'd given him.

10

Perry Mason was putting on his coat, preparing to leave his apartment, when the phone rang. He had arrived back from Las Vegas in the early hours of the morning and had had only a few hours' sleep.

As he reached to answer the phone, he glanced at the clock on a nearby table. The time was 8 A.M.

The woman's voice on the other end of the line was barely audible.

"Mr. Mason? Mr. Perry Mason?"

"Mason speaking."

"Mr. Mason, this is Laurel Adrian. I'm calling you from police headquarters. The police picked me up about an hour ago. They said I'm charged with killing my husband."

Mason shook his head silently in exasperation. He had hoped to make arrangements with Carter Phillips to surrender Laurel when a warrant was issued for her arrest. But he hadn't been able to reach the D.A. the previous day nor had Phillips returned any of his phone calls. Now he had to wonder if the D.A. hadn't been deliberately avoiding him. He also had to wonder why the police had taken Laurel into custody at such an early hour in the morning.

Despite his feelings, he kept his voice calm and reassuring when he answered her.

"I'll be there as quickly as I can. We'll arrange bail and have you out before midmorning. In the meantime, don't answer any questions. If anyone, and I mean anyone, attempts to discuss the case with you, you are to tell them I'm your attorney and all matters concerning your case should be taken up with me. Is that clear?"

"Yes. I understand." Her voice was stronger.

"Good. You just try to relax until I get there."

The morning was gray and overcast as Mason drove to police headquarters.

When a police matron brought Laurel Adrian into the interview room, he was pleased to note that although she was pale she appeared to be quite composed.

Still, there were faint traces of tears in her eyes when she smiled gratefully at him and said softly, "Thank you so much for being here."

He patted her hand. "It's going to be all right. Now, tell me exactly what happened this morning."

She shook her head as if bewildered. "The police came to the beach house, showed me a warrant for my arrest, and brought me here."

"You've not discussed the case with anyone here?"

"No. No, you told me not to."

"All right," Mason said briskly. "The matron will take you away while I make arrangements with a judge to release you on bail. A couple of hours is all it should take."

She nodded.

Mason signaled to the police matron waiting outside the glass partition of the interview room.

After Laurel was led away, Mason started to leave. He waited when Lieutenant Dallas came through the door.

"Good morning, Counselor."

"Yeah." Mason didn't feel friendly enough this day to give him more than that one word.

"Look," Dallas said placatingly, "I understand how you could feel we played a dirty trick on you and your client the way we snatched her up and brought her in this morning. But I didn't have any other choice."

"The other choice," Mason pointed out, "would have been to have phoned me and I'd have arranged to surrender her."

Dallas shook his head. "It couldn't have been done that way. The D.A. ordered it. When the new evidence turned up."

"What new evidence?"

"She didn't tell you? We told her."

"What new evidence?" Mason asked again, impatiently.

Dallas rubbed his forehead. "You remember the gun we found on the desk in Adrian's den. The thirty-eight?"

"The gun that killed him," Mason said, again impatiently.

Dallas spread his hands. "That's just it! Ballistics ran tests and says the bullets that killed him didn't come from the thirty-eight."

"What?" Mason was confounded.

"The bullets that killed Gilbert Adrian were fired from the thirty-two revolver that was in the desk drawer. The gun licensed to your client."

"I see" was all Mason said.

"The thirty-eight was the gun that killed the unidentified guy at the Oaks Restaurant. The two bullets in the wall of Adrian's den also came from the thirty-eight."

Mason absorbed the information without comment.

"Anyway," Dallas said sympathetically, "it's probably better we brought her in early and avoided all the reporters. And listen, Counselor, I've already checked for you and found out that Judge Albert Horman will be in court at ten A.M. for a bail hearing."

"All right, thanks. And what about the papers of indictment?"

The lieutenant made a motion with his thumb toward the door. "Assistant D.A. Al Marcus is waiting outside with them. I asked him to give me a minute alone with you."

"See you in court, Lieutenant," Mason said, putting a hand on the detective's shoulder as they left the interview room.

11

Two hours and forty-five minutes later Mason and Laurel Adrian stood on the outside steps of the courthouse.

"That wasn't *too* bad, was it?" Mason asked.

Laurel, who had been gazing upward at the sky, which was still overcast, lowered her head to look at him.

"Honestly, Mr. Mason, I was frightened to death for the first time since Gil was killed. Before, even though I knew they were going to arrest me, I just never really visualized myself in a courtroom." She shivered. "It was scary."

Mason smiled at her kindly. "Your reaction was to be expected. Today was your first experience with the power of the law of the land. It's meant to be intimidating to discourage wrongdoing. But you only have to remember that there are safeguards to keep it just. We'll see to it that all those safeguards are utilized to protect you."

"Yes," she said.

To Mason the bail hearing had been routine. He had read the indictment before they went into court and then had entered a plea of not guilty on Laurel's behalf to the one charge, second-degree murder. Judge Moorman had set bail of $500,000. Mason had argued for a lower amount but the judge had upheld the prosecution's contention for the higher sum. Laurel, who had sole ownership of the beach house, secured bail by a signature bond.

A date was set for a preliminary hearing.

At the bottom of the courthouse steps Mason asked Laurel, "Can I drive you somewhere? We should have a talk."

"Well, since I'm stranded anyway unless I can find a cab or the police would agree to take me back home, yes."

"No problem."

Mason had already phoned Della Street from the courthouse lobby, told her what was happening, and said it would be a while before he got to the office.

On the drive out to Malibu, in Mason's car, he said, "There are a couple of things that aren't clear in my mind. Do you feel we can discuss them?"

"I'm all right now," Laurel answered. She was settled into the seat beside him.

"All right, then. First, I'd like you to tell me about the gun. Your gun. Who else knew it was in the desk drawer?"

"Gil did, of course. I don't know who else."

"The police have determined the gun was wiped clean. No fingerprints on it."

"I guess whoever used it to kill Gil would have done that. All I know is that I put it in the desk drawer a long time ago."

Mason looked at her sharply. "Now we come to Randolph Adrian, and this is very important. He's going to testify that your husband was killed one day before he planned to change his will."

"I don't know why the fact that Gil planned to change his will should be any great surprise. I assumed he would. After all, we were getting divorced and we'd agreed on a property settlement. Why wouldn't he eliminate me from his will?"

"Then you did know that you were in his will?"

"He had told me so, yes."

Mason frowned. "It's the implication of *when* he planned to do it. He was cutting you out of the will and a day before he planned to do it, he was killed."

"But I didn't know about his plan," Laurel protested.

"He didn't tell you?"

"He had been out of the habit of confiding anything to me for a long time, Mr. Mason."

"You must be absolutely certain about this matter," Mason said sternly. "Absolutely certain no one else told you about his plans, either. If I try to shake Randolph's testimony on this point and then the D.A. is able to bring out that you did know, it could be damning to your defense."

She looked straight at him. "There's no way anyone can prove I knew of his plans because I didn't know. It's that simple."

"All right." Mason took from his pocket the picture of the man who had been shot and killed at the Oaks Restaurant. "Did you ever see this man?"

Laurel looked at the photograph of the dead man, looked at Mason, and shook her head.

"You're sure? This is the man witnesses say was shot by your husband at the Oaks Restaurant just before your husband returned home and was himself shot."

"I've never seen him before."

Mason returned the photograph to his pocket.

Laurel was silent for a moment before she touched the sleeve of his jacket. "I have a question. What exactly happens next? I mean I know there's going to be a preliminary hearing but I don't really understand what that means."

Mason quickly explained to her that at the preliminary hearing there would be a judge but no jury. The purpose of the hearing would be for the prosecution to present enough evidence to persuade the judge that there was sufficient reason to bring her to trial.

"Of course, we will have the right to contest the evidence and prove your innocence," he added.

"And that could be the end of it?" Laurel asked. "I mean if the judge is convinced I'm innocent?"

Mason explained to her that at a preliminary hearing the defense had a choice of simply taking advantage of an opportunity to discover such evidence as the prosecution might have which might be contested at a later jury trial. "Or," he said, "we can go into the preliminary hearing with an all-out defense, with our own evidence and witnesses, and try to end the case against you. You and I must decide."

"Do it!" she said emphatically.

"Not so fast," Mason said. "I want us to agree on our strategy but I don't want you to make this judgment based solely on your emotional feelings. Or a desire to end the whole business as quickly as possible."

"I trust you," she said. "Convince me of what your judgment is, either way."

He nodded. "All right. Yes, I'm inclined to believe we should put on our strongest defense at the preliminary hearing. I think we already know most of the major evidence the prosecution has to offer. I think we can counter it with our own evidence and witnesses and at least plant in the judge's mind the certainty that no jury will find you guilty beyond a reasonable doubt."

"Do it!" she repeated.

"There's only one risk."

"What's that?"

He looked at her probingly. "That the prosecution may produce some surprise evidence or witness at the last moment."

Her answer was firm. "I don't know how that would be possible, Mr. Mason."

"Okay, we're agreed then."

As she got out of the car at the beach house, Mason said, "There's one more thing I think you should know, Laurel. I have reason to believe the police are keeping surveillance on you. Or were. They may have called it off now that you've been indicted. But you should be aware of the possibility."

She looked at him for a moment as if she was startled by his words. She said, "Yes, I'll keep it in mind."

He left her with a reminder to keep in close touch with his office.

12

"And that's the whole story," Mason said, concluding his account of the trip to Las Vegas and his meeting with Anselmo Costa.

"Okay," Lieutenant Dallas said. "So you got the name of the guy Adrian shot. Let's see it."

Mason took from his pocket the piece of paper on which he'd written the name and address recorded in the hotel register. He placed the paper, which was folded in half, on the restaurant table in front of Dallas.

Mason said, "Before you look at it, I'll wager the name and address are both phony."

Dallas grinned. "I'm afraid I'm not tempted to take that wager."

He opened the paper, read it, and looked up. "It's the same phony name and address he used on his driver's license. You'd win the wager."

Mason sighed. "As I suspected. Costa's a wily one. He had answers for everything. But there *was* a connection between him and Adrian and this man, whoever he was. At least I established that much."

"Can I ask you a question?"

"Shoot."

"Suppose you had found out the dead man's true identity and that he had a connection with Costa and Adrian, what would you expect the police to do with the information?"

"Check it out, of course," Mason said.

"And how would that help your client? You know, and I know, as we've discussed before, the man Adrian shot couldn't in turn have killed Adrian."

Mason pointed a finger. "If the man *was* a hit man, and I think he was, as I believe you do, take it one step further."

Dallas shook his head. "What? I don't follow you."

Before Mason could answer, the waiter brought their steak sandwiches.

As they started to eat, Mason said, "There could have been a second hit man. One who shot and killed Adrian."

Dallas frowned. "I think you're reaching, Counselor."

"Perhaps. But it could explain how Adrian could have been shot so quickly after he left the restaurant and went home. The second hit man could have followed him, shot him, and gotten away before either Laurel Adrian or the police arrived at the house."

"It would explain that fact," the lieutenant agreed. "But not how the library was ransacked before Adrian was shot."

"Forget that for the moment. I think you're missing my point."

"Tell me."

"I think," Mason said, "the prosecution is so convinced that my client killed Adrian, nobody's ever looked in another direction or considered any other possibility."

He grinned. "Maybe, too, you should stop and wonder if I'm not trying to do you a favor."

"Do me a favor, how?"

"If during the course of the trial I start to develop evidence that someone other than Laurel Adrian is the murderer, it certainly won't make you look good, particularly if I establish the fact that you didn't try to find anyone else."

Dallas said, "All you're telling me is that you're planning to introduce the elements of reasonable doubt into the trial. I al-

ready assumed that would be your strategy. I'd guess Carter
Phillips assumes so, as well."

Mason smiled. He knew they were just having a friendly verbal
joust.

"You can't say I didn't try to present you with a possibility that
someone other than Laurel Adrian is the murderer."

Dallas smiled, too. He put down his knife and fork. "Tell you
what I'm going to do, just to prove I have an open mind. Off the
record, I'll do some digging around, see if I can find some evidence that might tie Costa in to the case, whether there was one
hit man or two."

"That's all I ask, Ray. But I have to warn you: He's as slick as a
fox with greased fur, and as sly."

"I'll keep that in mind," Dallas said. "What about Drake? I
mean, is he okay after his encounter in Las Vegas?"

"As a matter of fact, he's meeting me here." Mason glanced at
his watch. "He should be along anytime now. The Las Vegas
police dismissed all charges against him. And I think he's pretty
well recovered from the working-over he received."

"Glad to hear it."

They finished their lunch and Paul Drake, Jr., appeared. Melanie Sandford, the blackjack dealer from The Palms Palace in Las
Vegas, was with him.

Mason introduced Dallas to Melanie; Dallas shook hands with
Drake, settled his dinner check with Mason, dutch treat, as was
their custom, and left the restaurant.

Drake and Melanie sat down at the table with Mason.

Melanie Sandford certainly had the looks to be a dancer instead
of a blackjack dealer in Las Vegas, Mason thought, as he looked at
her sitting at the table. She was a pert, auburn-haired young
woman in her twenties with a sparkling smile and bright green
eyes.

"Perry," Drake said, "we have some news for you."

"All right." Mason turned his attention from Melanie to Drake.
"Let's hear it, Paul."

"Joe Lennart found an apartment for Melanie to stay in, not far
from his place. Earlier today, Joe, Melanie, and I were looking
over some of the earlier stories that appeared in the newspapers

about Adrian." Drake paused and turned to Melanie. "You tell him."

"Well," she said, "there were all these pictures of people they said were involved with Mr. Adrian—"

Paul interrupted, "She means at the time Adrian was indicted."

Melanie nodded. "And there was this one photograph I recognized." She put an open newspaper page on the table. "Her."

Mason saw that the photograph was of Councilwoman Janet Coleman.

"Go on," Mason said.

"I didn't know her name when I saw her in Las Vegas," Melanie said. "But it was her all right. I saw her there more than once with Mr. Adrian."

"You're sure it was her?"

"Yes. I'm positive."

"Tell him the rest," Drake said.

"And I saw her with Mr. Costa a lot, too. Sometimes the three of them would be together, sometimes she'd come in with just Mr. Costa to gamble."

"I may need you to testify to what you've just told me." Mason looked at her carefully. "Would that bother you?"

Melanie shook her head. "I wouldn't be bothered. Mr. Drake already told me that you might want to use me as a witness. What I'd say is the truth."

Mason gave her a reassuring smile. "You could be a help."

"Then I'd like that," Melanie said firmly.

"Thank you very much, Melanie." Mason smiled again.

Drake stood. "Joe's waiting in the car outside, Perry. I'll just see Melanie to the door. I'll be right back."

Mason watched Drake walk Melanie to the door of the restaurant, wait there briefly after she'd gone out, and then return to the table.

"Nice work, Paul," Mason said as Drake sat down again.

Drake nodded. "She's a nice kid, too. We probably did her a favor, getting her out of the casino. She says now she wants to find a job here in L.A."

"She's not Joe Lennart's girlfriend, is she?"

"No." Drake winked at Mason. *"I'm* the one who's been seeing her since we got back to town. Joe's keeping an eye on her, in case

Costa should send someone looking for her. She did leave her job rather abruptly and Costa may have already put two and two together and figured we were the ones who spirited her away."

Mason leaned back in his chair. "Paul, the fact that Melanie's seen Janet Coleman with Costa in Las Vegas certainly suggests a possible new angle to things. Maybe, just maybe, if a hit man did go gunning for Gil Adrian he was hired by Janet Coleman instead of Costa. And if there were two hit men, maybe she hired the second one as well."

"It could have happened," Drake agreed. "Janet Coleman had a lot to lose if Adrian had lived to go to trial. By the way, what did Lieutenant Dallas have to say when you told him about our encounters with Costa?"

"He's going to do some digging around unofficially. Now I wish I'd waited to talk to him so I could have told him about Janet Coleman as well."

Mason glanced at his watch. It was still early afternoon. He asked, "Paul, did any of your men get a line on that house in the Adrian neighborhood where the earlier robbery and murder took place?"

Drake nodded. "I left a report on your desk."

"I haven't been in the office today," Mason said.

Drake took out a notebook. "One of my operatives checked it out at the local precinct. You were right; it was never solved. The police listed it as a routine breaking and entering in the course of which the owner of the house was shot and killed. The owner's name was Martin Burress. The address is Five-five-six Elmwood Drive. The widow still lives there."

Mason stood up abruptly. "Good. Let's take a drive out there. Just maybe the police have overlooked a connection between the two cases." He was already moving out the door. Drake had to hurry to catch up with him.

Mason, in the car, cut in and out of the slow-moving flow of traffic leading out on the Santa Monica Freeway to the hills.

The Burress house was typical of the other houses on the streets of the neighborhood where Gilbert Adrian had lived. The house was three stories high and set behind a high, well-kept hedge.

When Mason, with Drake beside him, rang the bell, the door

was opened by a pretty young Hispanic woman wearing a white apron.

Mason took one of his business cards from his pocket and handed it to the woman as he said, "If Mrs. Burress is in, please tell her I'd like to speak to her."

The woman nodded her head. "I'll see."

The door closed and Mason and Drake had a short wait before the door opened again, and a tall, quite elegant-looking woman stood there. Mason surmised that she was in her early sixties, her gray hair soft around a face that was still attractive.

"Mr. Mason?" she asked. "You wished to see me? I'm Kathleen Burress."

Mason smiled affably. "I'm representing a client, Mrs. Laurel Adrian—"

"Yes, yes, I know who you are," Kathleen Burress interrupted, "and about the case involving your client. Why is it you wish to talk to me?"

Mason said carefully, "Because I have heard of the unfortunate incident that occurred here at your house six months ago."

"You mean the robbery? The murder of my husband?"

"Yes."

She looked at him, her eyes narrowed. "You think there's a connection between the shooting of my husband and the murder of Gilbert Adrian?"

"Let's just say I'd like to satisfy myself on the point, one way or the other."

"So would I, Mr. Mason. So would I," she said to his surprise and opened the door wide. "Please come in."

Mason introduced Drake to Mrs. Burress as they entered the house.

She led them across a hallway to a spacious drawing room bright with vases of fresh-cut flowers and with paintings by old masters hanging on the walls. The floor-to-ceiling windows looked out over an expanse of green lawn enclosed by the high hedge.

When they were seated, Mrs. Burress said quickly, "I would never have expected you to seek me out after I read of the Adrian murder in the neighborhood but I'm glad you did."

"Why is that?" Mason asked.

"Because," she said impatiently, "I made several attempts at talking to the police about a connection between the two cases and I received the impression they weren't even interested in considering the possibility."

"Who did you talk to?"

"Lieutenant Latham. Frank Latham. He was in charge of the investigation of my husband's murder, so I thought he would be the logical person to contact. I made several phone calls to him and even went to see him at the station house. He listened politely enough but I could tell he really wasn't giving it much thought."

"But you have," Mason prompted.

She nodded. "Oh, yes. Right from the moment I first learned of Gilbert Adrian's murder, I wondered: Could it have been the work of the same person who broke in here and shot Mr. Burress?"

"Were there similarities between the two incidents?" Drake asked. "That is, based upon what you've learned about the murder of Adrian?"

"Definitely," she said. "The night our house was broken into we were both out, separately. When I arrived, the police were here. Neighbors had heard the sounds of the gunshots and called the police. My husband was dead on the floor in the library. Someone had broken in through one of the French doors and made off with jewelry and several small antiques after shooting my husband. He must have walked in on them in the middle of the robbery. Or at least that's what the police told me they believed."

Mason asked gently, "Did the police ever indicate to you that they had any possible leads in the case?"

"Not exactly that, no," Mrs. Burress said. "But I will tell you that at first I was sure they would catch whoever did it. They seemed to be working so hard on the case, especially Lieutenant Latham. I mean for weeks he was here in the neighborhood almost daily, questioning people living on the streets all around."

"Did you ever talk to any of those people, the ones he was questioning?" Mason asked. "Did they ever give you any idea of the kinds of questions he asked?"

She nodded. "Oh, yes. People told me he wanted to know if they'd noticed any strangers around at the time of the murder. If anyone who had worked at any of the houses had quit after it happened, things like that."

She paused and thought for a moment. "I even met Laurel Adrian at that time. She came to call to offer her condolences after the lieutenant had been to question her. And I talked with her again when I heard from several of my friends that hers was one of the houses Lieutenant Latham had returned to to ask additional questions. I tried to find out if she perhaps had given him a possible lead."

"And had she?" Mason asked.

Mrs. Burress shook her head. "She told me that she didn't know of anything she had told the lieutenant that could have helped the investigation. I gather from what she told me, and from what others said, that he requestioned certain individuals in the hope that they might have remembered something they had forgotten to tell him."

She smiled sadly and sighed. "After a while I didn't see Lieutenant Latham or any of the police, nor did I hear from them. It seemed they had just run into a dead end. I'm afraid I decided the case would never be solved. And I gave up all hope. Then, when Gilbert Adrian was shot just a few doors away, well, I thought, now maybe the police will look into my husband's murder again."

She looked at Mason and Drake as if seeking some hope.

"I can't really assure you of that," Mason said. "But I can tell you we'll be doing some checking of our own. And if we find out anything, we'll inform you. Thank you for talking with us."

"Mr. Mason, Mr. Drake, I assure you that I thank *you*. At least I'll know that the death of my husband hasn't been forever forgotten and there's no chance that the killer of Mr. Burress will ever be brought to justice."

Mason was silent and thoughtful when he and Drake drove away from the Burress house.

Finally Drake asked, "What do you think, Perry?"

"On the one hand," Mason said, "it may well be that the police have good reason to believe there's no possible connection between the two murders."

"Let's hear what's on the other hand."

"This Lieutenant Latham may have caught onto something in

the very beginning that has escaped the rest of the Police Department, including Ray Dallas."

"And what would that be?" Drake asked, curious.

Mason said, "That whoever broke into the Burress house and killed Martin Burress made a mistake."

"A mistake?"

Mason nodded. "That whoever it was was supposed to break into Adrian's house, and got the two houses mixed up."

"If Latham believed that, it could explain why he kept returning to Adrian's house, talking to Laurel, at the time of the first break-in and murder," Drake said.

"Yep." Mason nodded.

"So now we see what we can find out from the lieutenant?"

"Nope." Mason grinned. "We'll let him alone for now. And I'm not going to mention anything about him to Ray Dallas. Maybe Latham will surprise all of us."

13

City Councilwoman Janet Coleman, in person, as opposed to newspaper photographs, had a potentially fatal lure for any male whose path she crossed, Mason decided upon his first sight of her.

She was coming out of City Hall at lunchtime, neat from her patent-leather pumps up her long legs to her tailored suit, silk blouse, coral necklace, face shaped over classic bones, all topped by tawny hair.

Mason was waiting in front of the building where she had told him she'd meet him when he'd phoned and asked if they might have a talk.

She came directly to him, hand outstretched, and said, "Mr. Mason, I'm Janet Coleman."

He knew she meant to flatter him by recognizing him at sight. He admitted to himself that he *was* flattered.

He started to say, "I know a good restaurant nearby—" but she interrupted.

"Lunch is on me." She raised a hand holding a large cardboard carton tied with string. "The day is too beautiful to eat indoors. I took the liberty of ordering us lunch from my favorite gourmet deli. All I didn't do is reserve us a bench in the park. Are the arrangements okay with you?"

Mason had to laugh. "Indeed."

In the park, she found them an empty bench off by itself, put the cardboard carton between them and opened it. She took out paper plates, silverware, cloth napkins, two pewter mugs, a small thermos of coffee, tiny containers of cream and of sugar, pâté, pieces of chicken, potato salad, and a green salad.

"I like it here at lunchtime," she said, nibbling at the pâté. "I often come alone to clear out all the cobwebs."

"It's certainly different and I like the food, the service, and the atmosphere."

"Yes." She poured them both some coffee and looked up. "You don't know this, Mr. Mason, but I've been following your trial cases ever since I was in law school, at UCLA. I've even been a spectator in the courtroom during some of your most famous cases."

"You had planned to be a lawyer?" Mason asked.

"A criminal lawyer," she said. "I wanted to do what you've always done, defend the accused."

"What happened to sidetrack you?"

"A combination of small circumstances." She paused and laughed. "Plus impatience and ambition. I was sidetracked into politics and discovered I like politics—except for the bureaucracy. Anyhow, I wanted you to know that you were someone I always admired."

She tilted her head to one side. "I'll bet right now you're thinking, 'Ah, she's pulling out all the stops to charm me.'"

Mason shrugged. "You're very direct, Miss Coleman. And, yes, charming."

"The truth is, everything I've said to you is so."

"My response then would have to be: I thank you."

"Now then"—she touched a napkin to her lips—"I imagine you'd like to get on with the matter you wanted to discuss with me, the murder of Gil Adrian."

"Yes."

"I'm afraid that what I have to say is going to be a disappointment to you, particularly if you think I have any information as to who killed him. And, also, because you'd be limited in the questions you could ask me."

Mason reflected briefly that she was a remarkably self-assured young woman, considering that she had been involved with Adrian and rumored to be a principal figure in his alleged bribery of public officials.

What he said to her was "Why is that, Miss Coleman?"

She glanced around carefully before she said softly, "You see, Mr. Mason, the fact is, for the past year or more I have been working undercover for the federal government in its probe of the city officials who took payoffs from Adrian. Dave Niles said I could talk to you with the understanding that you won't reveal any of this."

Mason was astonished. "You mean you weren't really involved with Adrian, romantically or in his alleged illegal activities?"

Still speaking softly, she said, "I was not, no. I was, I am, part of the federal prosecutor's team. I volunteered for the undercover assignment when I was approached. My supposed romantic connection with him was only part of my cover. All of this would of course have been revealed if he had lived to go on trial. Even now, you understand, the bribery case is not closed. There will be indictments and I will testify in them as one of the government's chief witnesses. You see why you can't use me in your trial?"

Mason sat back on the park bench. "Well—it certainly explains one thing."

"What's that?"

"As soon as I met you today, I wondered how in the world a person like you could be mixed up with someone like him and his shady dealings." Mason smiled at her.

"Now it's my turn to say thank you," she said. She touched his coat sleeve with her hand. "Do you really think you can get her acquitted?"

"Laurel Adrian, you mean? Yes, I do."

"And you're sure she didn't kill him."

"I don't believe it, no." He shook his head.

"From what I've heard," Janet Coleman said, "the prosecution can establish motive, means, and opportunity. That's a powerful combination."

"All circumstantial."

"Still." She leaned forward. "What can I do to help?"

"Tell me about Gil Adrian."

"He was arrogant, greedy, utterly ruthless with other people. That last, in fact, was how I first came to know him. He bought a building in my council district and began immediately to harass the tenants. He wanted to force them out so he could demolish the building and put up a highrise."

"And did he succeed?"

"The tenants formed a committee and took him to court," she said. "I gave them my support. The case is still tied up in the courts. But as soon as he discovered I was working on the tenants' behalf, he began to try to con me with his charms. It was then that I was asked to work undercover for the government, agreed, and encouraged him in his attentions to me."

"I imagine that could have been risky for you if he had found out what you were really doing," Mason said.

"It was a risk but I thought it was worth it."

"Tell me about Anselmo Costa in Las Vegas. I believe you were acquainted with him."

She laughed. "You really have been digging, haven't you?"

Mason said quietly, "Sometimes that's how you bring up the rocks—and what's underneath them."

"Well put. I like that, Mr. Mason. What I was able to determine is that there was some kind of connection between Costa and Gil and the casino. But I was never able to find out exactly what it was."

"I'd be curious to know if you developed any theories about them."

"Nothing that would hold up in court. But yes." She took a sip of coffee. "I think there were two connections. I think Costa was bankrolling Gil when Gil needed to get one of his projects off the ground, supplying Gil with the cash for the kickbacks. *And* I think they were using the casino to launder money. But I have no evidence."

Mason nodded, and took from his pocket the photograph of the man Adrian had shot.

"Did you ever see this man?"

She studied the photograph before she said, "No, never. I'm sure I haven't."

"He's the still-unidentified man Gil Adrian shot the night he himself was killed. There's some indication he was a hit man hired to eliminate Adrian, only Adrian shot him first."

She was impressed. "If you could prove that—"

Mason completed the sentence, "—it would show there were others capable of wanting Adrian dead. But I have discovered more than that."

"Tell me."

"I have a witness who will testify that she's seen Costa and this man together."

"I think I see what you're getting at," Janet Coleman said quickly. "If there was one hit man, there could have been a second."

"That's it." Mason was pleased.

"I wish I could help you," she said sincerely.

He smiled at her. "You have."

She gathered up the remains of their lunch and closed up the cardboard container.

Then she said, "Mr. Mason, there's something I want you to know. I've never met Laurel Adrian and Gil never talked about her at all. Even though my involvement was for entirely different reasons, I wouldn't want to believe I was the cause of their breakup. Nor do I."

"For what it's worth," Mason said, "I don't think you were, either. What's more, I think she's better off without him. Not that that would give her any right to kill him, which I feel certain she didn't."

"If you need me to testify within the limits we discussed, I'll be more than willing to do what I can."

She touched his hand and they separated in the park.

Mason walked back to his office, stopping in first at the Drake Detective Agency, which was just down the corridor from his own office.

The girl at the switchboard looked up expectantly, then said, "Hi, Mr. Mason."

"Hello, Jenny. Is Paul in?"

"Yes, he is."

"Anyone with him?"

"No, sir."

"Good, buzz him, tell him I'm on my way in," Mason said and, unlatching the gate in the partition, went through a veritable maze of offices, to tap on the door marked MANAGER PRIVATE.

"Come in, Perry, come in," Drake called out from inside.

Mason entered the office and Drake pulled over a chair for him and went back to his place behind the desk, asking, "How did it go with Madam Councilwoman Coleman?"

"Another lead that wound up at a dead end."

"Couldn't pry anything out of her, huh?"

"It's not that," Mason said. "She's okay. I really can't go into all the details about her for now. You'll have to take my word for it. But there's something else I want to talk to you about."

"Shoot."

Mason said, "I've been going over all the newspaper accounts of what was purported to have happened the night Adrian was killed and something in them caught my eye."

Mason rubbed his jaw reflectively. "It was something that restaurant owner, his name was John Fallon, reported to the police. He stated that when Adrian entered the restaurant that night Adrian went to the phone booth and made a call before he sat down at the table. And Fallon stated the time was close to nine P.M."

"I can guess what you want. To find out who Adrian called."

"It shouldn't be that difficult." Mason grinned. "I've now given you the date, the time, and the location of the origination of the call."

Drake grinned back. "So that all I have to do is get the phone number of the booth at the restaurant and then try to get somebody at the telephone company to give me the rest of it."

"For a man with your resources," Mason got up from the chair and started toward the door, "it should be easy."

Mason went along the corridor to his own office. When he opened the outer door Gertie, at the switchboard, looked up with obvious relief.

"Oh, Mr. Mason, am I glad to see you!" she said almost tearfully.

"What is it, Gertie?"

"A young woman came to see you. About an hour ago." Gertie's hands were fluttering nervously in the air. "She said it was of the utmost importance that she talk to you. And she wouldn't wait here in the reception area. She said it was too risky, and she wouldn't leave, either. I didn't know what to do. You and Della were both out."

He said, "So where is this person?"

"She wanted to wait in your office but I couldn't let her do that. So I put her in Della's office."

"You did exactly the right thing," he reassured her.

He went to Della's office and entered without knocking.

The young woman who was sitting, hands folded in her lap, was startled at his sudden appearance.

"Oh—" she said, "Mr. Mason. I'm so thankful you're here."

She stood up quickly. "I'm Megan Calder. I'm—I was—Mr. Gilbert Adrian's secretary. I thought I should speak to you about some matters you ought to know."

Megan Calder was a blonde, about medium height, a couple of pounds on the plump side, who looked to be in her late twenties. Her expression was solemn as if she was under some strain.

"Please sit down," Mason said, as he perched on the edge of Della's desk. "Tell me what I can do for you."

"I want to help Mrs. Adrian, Mrs. Laurel Adrian," the young woman said. "I read that you are her attorney." She paused.

Mason nodded encouragingly. "Go on, please."

"Well I—I thought you'd want to know about the safe Mr. Adrian had at his house." She paused again.

Mason nodded encouragingly once more.

She said in a rush of words, "He kept money there, cash, lots of it, in case he needed it in a hurry. I don't believe anyone else knew about that."

"I see."

"There was no mention in the news about any money disappearing so I don't think anyone knew about it. Am I right?"

"It certainly would seem so," Mason said thoughtfully.

"I don't think he meant for me to know but he let it slip once and I pretended I didn't hear."

"And you haven't told the police yet?"

She shook her head.

"Why did you come to me with this information?"

"I would like to help Laurel Adrian. I don't think she killed him. Would this information hurt her case?"

Mason answered quickly and brusquely, "Whether it would help her or hurt her, you must tell the police. See a Lieutenant Ray Dallas at Headquarters."

She nodded.

"I do appreciate your telling me this. I have to ask you a question, though: Are you and Laurel friends, by any chance?"

"Friends?" She seemed puzzled. "Oh, no. I hardly knew her at all, just to speak to whenever she came into the office. Which wasn't very often. Why—? Oh, I see, you thought maybe I'm trying to help her because we're friends. No, Mr. Mason."

Mason smiled. "All right."

"There's something else, too," Megan Calder said. She reached into a large manila envelope that was on the chair beside her and took out a leather-covered book. "After Mr. Adrian was murdered, I found this appointment book stuck away in the bottom of one of his desk drawers."

"Didn't the police come to the office after the murder?" Mason asked.

She avoided his eyes. "I guess they overlooked it."

Or you removed it before they arrived, Mason thought.

Mason took the book, leafed through the pages, and saw it was a day-by-day log of appointments with inked-in entries on every page.

He glanced up. "I take it this is a record of his appointments for the last year."

"More than that," she said, her face set in a deep frown. "It's a duplicate record of entries recorded in the appointment book he always kept on top of his desk, the only one I knew about until I found this one. There's something else, too."

She pointed to the page open in the book. "See, on one side are notations of his appointments for each day, lunches, meetings, dinner dates, and so on. They match the entries in his other appointment book, day by day, hour by hour. I checked. Now, notice, on the other side of the page—enclosed in parentheses— are entries here and there of other appointments that aren't included in the book he kept on his desk."

Mason was reading down the page. "Yes, I see."

"What's really strange," Megan Calder pointed out, "is that where the entries are made in parentheses they're still for the same exact time as the other list of appointments. I can't figure out what it means."

"Perhaps," Mason ventured, "when he had appointments that conflicted, he kept a record of them in this book until he could figure out which of the two appointments he could accommodate."

She shook her head forcefully. "If he was going to go to that much trouble, why wouldn't he have crossed out the entries of the appointments he didn't keep? It just makes no sense."

"It *is* curious. Is it possible that you could leave this with me for a while to mull over?"

"I don't see why not. As far as I know no one else even knows of the existence of this record. Only, would you please do me a personal favor?"

"If I can," Mason said. "Certainly."

"Promise you'll let me know first thing if you do decipher it. I've been going crazy trying to work out what it means."

Mason smiled. "I promise."

She handed him a piece of paper. "If you do want to get in touch with me, here's my home phone number and address. I think it's better that you not contact me at Adrian Enterprises. Besides, I'm not at all sure how much longer I'll be employed there."

"You have a problem there?"

"Only one," she said, standing to leave. "Randolph Adrian. We've never gotten along. I'm sure if he has anything to say about it, now that his father's gone, he'll be delighted to give me my walking papers. I hope I'll have another job before that happens."

She laughed suddenly. "Your receptionist must have thought I was some kind of nut when I got here today and wouldn't wait outside there. You see, I was afraid he, Randolph, just might show up and see me. I know he came to visit you once before. Will you please explain for me?"

"Of course."

Mason walked her out to the corridor and thanked her for coming to see him.

As he started back into the office, he thought: Score one for the defense; maybe, score two, if the secret appointment book could be found to have a sinister purpose.

He sat down at the desk and Della knocked on the door and came in.

She said, "I understand there was a small fracas in the office while I was out. Gertie told me. What was it all about?"

"Nothing to worry about," Mason said. "Gilbert Adrian's secretary, a young woman named Megan Calder, came to see me." He told Della of the discussion he'd had with the secretary and showed her the secret appointment book Adrian had left.

He said, "I've been trying to unravel the significance of these notations of duplicate appointments and getting nowhere."

"Let me take a look." Della came and peered over his shoulder.

Mason ran a finger down the page. "Here, for instance, at three-thirty on this date, he wrote in, 'Meeting with J. Turner,' and then, in parentheses, 'Ground-breaking ceremonies, Bellows Hse.,' meaning 'Bellows House,' I'd guess."

He shook his head in annoyance. "Could you kindly tell me why in the world he'd want a record of two different dates scheduled for the same hour?"

"I've heard of people keeping two sets of books to hide their true income," Della said. "But *this*, no, I've never heard of such a thing."

"It goes on like this throughout the book, with certain duplications at one time or another, but not for every notation of an appointment."

Mason sighed. "I suppose the words in parentheses could be some kind of coded record having nothing to do with the actual words. Oh, well, I'll just have to keep puzzling over it when I have more time."

She went to the chair where she had been sitting during the meeting and picked up her shorthand book.

"I'll get these notes typed up for you."

She started toward the door and stopped. "And will you please tell me what you're doing with your desk all cleared? Are you leaving for the day?"

"No, I'm not leaving for the day." He smiled. "I'm just trying some of the advice I gave Laurel; resting, clearing my mind, trying to keep my spirits up."

14

"He lives in the first house on the right," Drake said, pointing across the street from where he and Perry Mason were parked in the car.

"And you say he usually comes back in the late afternoon about this time?"

"Every afternoon for the past three afternoons that I've been tailing him. He leaves the house, goes to the races at Hollywood Park, comes home. He never wins. He must go for the sun."

Mason looked at the small house across the way, one of ten set in a bungalow court. There weren't too many such bungalow courts—so popular in the city a few decades earlier—still in existence in L.A. High rises had replaced them.

The man they were watching for was named Steven Benedict. Drake had managed to trace the phone call Gil Adrian had made from the Oaks Restaurant the night of his murder to a phone listed in Benedict's name at the bungalow-court address. Drake had put Benedict under surveillance for three days so he and Mason would have some idea of his background.

"Now you see why I didn't want you to see him alone?" Drake

was looking at the photograph Mason held in his hand. Drake had taken the photograph with a camera equipped with a telescopic lens on the first day he had followed Benedict.

"He looks like he could handle himself all right," Mason agreed, studying the photograph.

The man in the photograph was heavyset, with a bullet-shaped head, blond hair cropped short, and small, piggish-looking eyes.

Mason glanced up and down the street and over at the bungalow again, where all the shades were pulled down against the glare of the setting sun.

"Here he comes now!" Drake said sharply as a compact car turned the corner and parked at the curb in front of the bungalow court.

Benedict squeezed out of the car and, without looking in any direction except straight ahead, walked in long strides to the house and went inside.

"He's been the easiest subject I've ever tried to follow; he never glances to right, left, or behind," Drake said softly. "As you observed, Perry, he looks like a man who could handle himself, no matter what trouble came from any direction."

Mason nodded, and reached to open the car door. "Okay, Paul, let's go."

They walked side by side to the house and the door opened at Mason's first knock.

Steven Benedict stood like a dark shadow, just inside the doorway, the light dim in the room behind him.

"Mr. Steven Benedict?" Mason asked and held out one of his business cards. "I'm Perry Mason, an attorney, and this is my associate, Paul Drake. I wonder if we might have a word with you? It will only take a few minutes of your time."

"Yeah, okay, come on in."

Benedict moved away from the door and raised the shades at a couple of windows.

"I know who you are, Mason," Benedict said. "From the news. Have a seat." He motioned to Mason and Drake.

"Then you perhaps know I'm representing Mrs. Laurel Adrian in her trial for the murder of her husband."

"Yeah, I know."

"And perhaps, too, then, you know why I'm here."

A woman came into the room. She was slim, dark-haired, rather plain-faced, and a good many years younger than Benedict's middle age.

"What is it, Steve?" she asked.

"This is Mr. Perry Mason and Mr. Drake. They want to talk to me." He looked at the two men. "My wife, Sheila."

Mason and Drake stood and shook hands with Sheila Benedict.

"Can I fix you something?" she asked.

Both men said no.

Benedict said, "Honey, why don't you get me a beer?"

"Sure," she said and went away.

Benedict put a hand gingerly to his sunburned face. "Why don't you tell me?"

"It's in reference to a phone call Gil Adrian made to your number at about nine P.M. on the night of May eleventh."

Benedict moved his hand to the top of his close-cropped hair.

Sheila Benedict had come back into the room. She handed him a beer and sat down beside him on the sofa.

"May eleventh," Benedict repeated, frowning.

"Gil Adrian called your phone number that evening from the Oaks Restaurant." Mason paused and added, "It was the night he was shot and killed. You did know Gil Adrian, didn't you?"

"Steve, you remember, you—" Sheila Benedict started to say.

Benedict cut her off, saying, "I'm going to level with you, Mr. Mason, Mr. Drake. Yeah, I knew Gil Adrian. I was his personal bodyguard. Wait a minute."

He got up and motioned to his wife to follow him as he left the room.

He was back alone, a few minutes later. He handed Mason a wallet flipped open to show that he was a member of the security force at Adrian Enterprises.

"I've been doing security work for a lot of years now," he said. "About three months ago Adrian hired me as his personal bodyguard."

"And you did receive a phone call from him that night?" Mason had handed the wallet to Drake who had looked at the I.D. card and handed the wallet back to Benedict.

"He called me at nine o'clock, yeah." Benedict spread his

hands. "Nothing important. He just wanted to tell me I could have the next day off."

Benedict took a swallow of beer. "See, after he was killed and all, I didn't particularly want to go to the police. I mean, you can understand, it doesn't do too much for my business prospects for it to get out that I was supposed to be bodyguard to a guy who gets himself shot. You know?"

Mason nodded as if in agreement. "So you didn't go to the police?"

"I just told you why. Besides, I didn't know anything to tell them about his murder. I still don't. I didn't want to get involved."

"Doesn't it strike you as a bit odd, Mr. Benedict, that Adrian didn't want you with him when he met the man at the Oaks Restaurant that he shot? I would think if he was meeting someone like that he'd want you with him or nearby."

Benedict shrugged. "It might seem odd. But again you have to understand that he often went off and wouldn't want me with him. It happened when I was working for him."

Mason thought for a moment. "Did you work for Adrian or for his company?"

"I was paid by the company. They carried me as a member of the security force."

"While you were working as his bodyguard," Mason said, "did he ever indicate to you why he felt he needed a bodyguard? Did he ever mention anyone he feared?"

"He didn't, no. I got the feeling he wanted me around, just as a precaution," Benedict said. "Of course, when I began to find out all that stuff from the news that he was going to be indicted and all, I thought to myself, man, he *needs* a bodyguard."

Mason smiled slightly. "Tell me, did you ever meet Mrs. Adrian?"

Benedict shook his head. "But I did see her sometimes with him, at the office when she'd come in. Most of the time I worked for him I kept out of sight from other people. He wanted me to keep an eye on him, on things, but he didn't want the world to know he'd hired a bodyguard."

Mason stood up and so did Drake.

Mason said, "You realize, don't you, now that we've talked, I will probably subpoena you to testify at Mrs. Adrian's trial?"

"It's okay with me." Benedict took another drink of beer. "I don't mind telling what I told you. Which is all I know."

"By the way, are you still employed by Adrian Enterprises?"

"I wouldn't know." Benedict shook his head. "I never went back after he was shot. Like I said, I was hoping to stay clear of the whole thing. Besides, nobody there probably even missed me after he was killed."

"Thank you for your time," Mason said.

When he and Drake were back in Drake's car, Mason said, "What do you think, Paul?"

"Hard to say." Drake had his eyes on the road as he drove. "I'll be doing some more checking. But I guess there's one good thing about finding him."

"What's that?"

"He can testify for you that he was Adrian's bodyguard but Adrian never mentioned he was afraid of his wife killing him. That should be some small help for your case."

"Some small help, yep," Mason agreed.

That night Mason phoned Gil Adrian's secretary, Megan Calder, at her home, and said, "I need a favor."

"Sure, Mr. Mason."

"Could you check the office employment files and see what you can find out about a Steven Benedict?"

"Steven Benedict?"

"That's right. He says he worked as part of the security force up until the time Adrian was killed."

"I'll see what I can do," she said. "Only I have to tell you something, Mr. Mason; you sure cut it close for me to get you the information."

"Why's that?" Mason asked.

"As I suspected and told you last week when we talked, I was given my notice of dismissal. By Randolph. Tomorrow's my last day."

"I'm sorry about that, Megan."

"Oh, don't worry about me, Mr. Mason. I'll be all right."

Mason hung up the phone. Megan Calder, he thought, was—in the words Della Street would use—another spunky one.

15

Perry Mason had come into the office early and was trying to get away to meet with Laurel Adrian on the eve of the opening of her pretrial hearing, but the phone kept ringing.

Megan Calder, on the phone, said, "I was able to obtain the information you wanted on Steven Benedict. According to the company files, he *was* carried on the payroll of the security staff, but reported only to Gil Adrian. Is that of any assistance to you?"

"Very much so."

He thanked her and she wished him good luck.

He disconnected the line and Della tapped on the door and stuck her head in.

"Perry, Gertie has several calls waiting for you, all newspaper and TV reporters asking if you have any statements to make about the hearing."

Mason glanced down at the day's newspapers spread across his desk. All carried front-page stories on the pretrial hearing that was about to begin.

He shook his head. "Tell them I'm out of the office and can't be reached for the rest of the day."

He stood up, carrying his briefcase. "Which won't be an untruth. By the time you get back to the phone, I'll be gone."

The sky above the city was gray and overcast as Mason drove out to Laurel's beach house, and then the sky began to brighten as he got closer to the ocean, where the sun had begun to burn away the overcast.

Laurel was expecting him and had set out coffee and a bowl of fruit. She was dressed casually in slacks and blouse and he thought how young and vulnerable she appeared. He was glad he had decided to have this final conversation with her before the hearing in the informality of the beach house.

"I'm really glad to see you, Mr. Mason," she said gratefully. "Alone here and reading the newspapers and watching the TV news about the hearing, I begin to feel as if I'm some person other than myself. Almost as if I were two people; the one in the news, the other the same person I've always been and am."

"Being in the spotlight of the media can have that effect," he assured her. "In a sense you are, for the moment, two different people. One a creation of the media, the other the same person you've always been. There's no way it can be otherwise until you can put the whole business behind you."

Mason leaned toward her. "Laurel, I'm going to do my very best for you starting tomorrow. There will be times when you may feel everything's going against you. Particularly at the beginning when the prosecution presents its case against you. Just keep reminding yourself that my turn will come to speak in your defense. Will you do that?"

"I'll try, Mr. Mason."

"You do that." He opened his briefcase. "There've been a couple of new developments since we talked last." He showed her the photograph Drake had taken of Steven Benedict.

"This man was apparently hired by your husband as a personal bodyguard. His name is Steven Benedict. I managed to verify that he was carried on the Adrian Enterprises' payroll as part of the security force. Can you recall ever having seen him?"

Laurel looked at the photograph for a long time. She shook her head.

"No, I don't recognize him. But there is something familiar about him. You know the feeling? As if perhaps I saw him at some time, in passing, without really registering when or where it was."

"That could be possible," Mason said. "Benedict claims your husband ordered him to stay in the background. Perhaps you saw him along with other people around your husband."

"I guess maybe that could be it."

"I expect to call him as a witness."

Mason took out a thick folder. "These are the documents assembled by the district attorney in preparation for your pretrial hearing. The law requires the D.A.'s office to supply such information to us, the defense, including the names of witnesses to be called and a record of their statements."

"I understand," Laurel said.

Mason said, "I've carefully reviewed the material and made notes of certain matters I want to check with you."

Laurel nodded.

"This shouldn't be too painful for you." Mason smiled to put Laurel at ease. "There don't seem to be any surprises among the witnesses the prosecution intends to call to testify."

Laurel, looking at him intently, moistened her lips with her tongue and waited.

Mason glanced down at his notes. "Tell me about your neighbor across the street from your house in the hills, a Mrs. Margaret Starke.

"They're going to call her as a witness? Why?"

"As part of their routine investigation following the murder, the police questioned various of your neighbors."

Laurel appeared perplexed. "But I don't even know her, except by name."

"Nevertheless, she told the police she heard you and your husband quarreling on several occasions," Mason said.

"But that's ridiculous! I mean, certainly she may have heard us exchange words—as all married couples do, I would imagine— but what does that have to do with my case?"

As gently as possible, Mason said, "The D.A. means to make her testimony a part of the record. Don't worry about it. But I do need your answer to my question. Tell me about Mrs. Starke."

"Yes, all right." Laurel sat up straighter in the chair. "I don't, however, like to say what I have to say. It's going to sound, you know, so self-serving."

Mason said sternly, "Look here, Laurel! This is no time for niceties. You're going to defend yourself against a murder charge. You'd better be self-serving. If you're not, at all times, I certainly can't save you. And neither can anyone else. Now, tell me about Mrs. Starke."

"She's never been friendly since the day we moved into that house," Laurel said. "And it was because of the actions of her husband."

"What about her husband?"

Laurel hesitated and said, "Right from the first he started paying undue—well, attention—to me. I didn't even realize it, I thought he was just being neighborly. But Gil noticed it. Gil sure did notice it."

She nodded her head in emphasis. "Her husband, Teddy, kept running over every time I was outside and Gil was away. Several times Gil came home and there Teddy Starke would be, following me around while I was tending the flowers or watering the lawn. As soon as Gil would appear Teddy would duck out. I guess I was naïve. And every time it happened Gil would be furious and yell about it in a voice loud enough for the Starkes to hear across the street."

She paused and added wistfully, "Gil was very attentive to me in those early days of our marriage. Anyhow, I guess that's when she heard us quarreling. Then, when she'd hear Gil, they, the Starkes, would have a big row and you could hear her all over the neighborhood telling him to stay away from me."

"Very good." Mason grinned. "That's what I needed to hear to deflate her testimony."

He glanced down at his notes again. "Does the name Angie Ryerson mean anything to you?"

She thought for a moment and said, "No. I don't think so."

"She's a teenager who lives a couple of blocks away from you in the hills."

"No, I'm not familiar with the name."

Mason said, "On the night of your husband's murder, she was baby-sitting for the family who live on the corner of your block, the Hendrens."

Laurel shook her head. "I don't know the family or the teenager. Is it important?"

"Well, she says she saw you get home that evening at eight P.M."

"No, no, she couldn't have. She's simply mistaken."

Mason looked at the copy of the teenager's statement.

"She says she knows who you are and knows your car."

"I'm sorry, Mr. Mason, I don't care what she says; she's wrong. Absolutely."

Mason nodded his head. "I'll have to see what I can do with her when she's on the stand."

"The other witnesses the D.A. plans to call are those who will give evidence observed at the crime scene or in the forensic laboratories later, and of your police interrogation. Lieutenant Dallas, the medical examiner, the ballistics expert, a couple of others who were present at the Oaks Restaurant when your husband was there earlier will testify."

"All those people!" Laurel said wonderingly. "All the statements they'll make to try to prove I'm guilty. It seems almost impossible anyone hearing all of them could ever believe I'm not guilty."

"You mustn't think of it that way," Mason said. "Your hearing will take place to try to determine the truth."

"And do you plan to call me to testify?"

"I don't know yet. We'll make that decision later when we see how the proceedings are going."

"I'd like to take the stand if you want me to." Her voice was determined. "You mustn't try to spare me simply because you know it would be an ordeal."

"I'd never hesitate on that account," Mason assured her. "I will make my decision on the basis of whether or not your testimony is needed."

She nodded.

He thought for a moment before he spoke.

"Laurel, the biggest problem I'm going to have is to find an explanation for how your husband had time, between leaving the restaurant and when he was shot, to virtually ransack his den. You can be certain D.A. Phillips is going to box me in on that point."

"I wish I could help you."

"What might help," Mason said, "is if you can recall the questions the police asked you and your answers. For instance, did they ask if you had had occasion to look into the den earlier that day?"

"No, I'm sure they didn't." She shook her head. "What they did ask was if I had opened the safe, destroyed some of his papers. I said I hadn't."

"And you're sure they didn't question whether or not you had seen the inside of the room earlier that day?"

"I'm sure. What difference would it have made if I had—if I had seen the room earlier?"

"Just that," he told her, "if you had been there earlier and everything was in order, then whoever went through the safe and the desk had to have done it that day. On the other hand, if you didn't look into the room that day, it's at least conceivable the disorder could have occurred the day before."

"I see." She frowned. "I am just unable to recall whether I was there earlier that day. I don't always go into the den. It was more Gil's room."

Mason said, "All right. The fact that you weren't questioned on the point could be of help to me."

He picked up his briefcase. "I suggest you stop reading the papers and watching TV. I'll see you tomorrow at nine."

She waved to him from the steps of the house when he was in his car headed back to the city.

He wished he could shake the feeling that throughout the case so far she had withheld something, some bit of information, from him. He could only hope whatever it was it wouldn't surface sometime during the hearing and destroy her defense.

16

Judge Andrew Moorman swept his eyes across the crowd gathered in the courtroom and said, "This is the time fixed for the preliminary hearing in the case of the People versus Laurel Adrian."

"Ready for the People," D.A. Carter Phillips said.

"Ready for the defendant," Perry Mason responded.

Mason settled back in his seat while the court clerk was swearing in the first witness called by the prosecution, John Fallon, manager of the Oaks Restaurant.

Mason watched District Attorney Carter Phillips approach the witness stand.

The D.A. was short and stocky with a thick mane of black hair combed back from a high forehead, a man who projected an attitude of great deliberateness in gesture and speech.

"Mr. Fallon, I am going to ask you a series of questions relating to a period of time directly before the murder of Gilbert Adrian," Phillips said, more to provide an explanation to the judge of what he was doing than to the witness.

Mason knew he could have raised an objection to the sequence in which the prosecution's witnesses were being presented; normally the first testimony should pertain to the scene of the crime, evidence that the murder had been committed. But he decided to let the opportunity pass. The judge might, after an explanation by Phillips of why Fallon had been called first, overrule the objection. More important, Mason believed, was to reserve his objections for times when he could disconcert or discredit the witness rather than the prosecutor. Mason had a theory that while a preliminary hearing in a courtroom was indeed like a play in a theater, with the judge and spectators as the audience, there was also an important difference between the two. While the attorneys for the prosecution and the defense were always in sight onstage at all times, they were only the directors of the drama; the witnesses were the stars of the proceedings, one after another.

John Fallon, on the witness stand, repeated the account, which Mason knew by heart, of Gil Adrian's visit to the Oaks Restaurant, of the shooting outside, of the time Adrian sped away in his car.

"And you are absolutely certain of the time Gilbert Adrian left your restaurant?" Phillips asked.

"Absolutely."

The D.A. turned away from the witness stand. "Cross-examine," he said to Perry Mason.

Mason said, "The defense reserves the right to call this witness back at a later time."

Judge Andrew Moorman had been leaning back in his chair at the bench during the examination of John Fallon. The judge, who was in his seventies, had a reputation for keeping proceedings moving. He glanced up over his spectacles at Carter Phillips.

"Call your next witness."

Police Lieutenant Frank Latham took the stand.

Mason listened intently as Carter Phillips led the lieutenant through the details of the arrival of the police at the Adrian house in the hills.

Latham testified to the time. He told of observing Laurel Adrian walking away from the front door toward her car. He stated how they had entered the house and found Adrian's body in the den, the .38-caliber revolver on the desk, the papers littering the floor, the open safe, the .32 revolver that Laurel Adrian had identified as hers in the desk drawer.

"Lieutenant," the D.A. said, "first, let's dispose of a certain matter you mentioned in your testimony. When you confronted Laurel Adrian outside her house that night, she told you she hadn't entered the house because she had lost her keys? Is that right?"

"That's right."

"And, later, did she find them?"

"Yes, sir. In the interior of her car."

The D.A. nodded, went to the prosecution table, picked up an envelope, and came back to position himself in front of the witness stand.

"I show you these photographs." Carter Phillips handed three photographs to Lieutenant Latham. "Is this the exact way the scene in the den looked on the night of the murder?"

Latham looked at the photographs.

"Yes."

He passed out copies of the photographs to the judge, and to Mason.

Mason glanced at the photographs.

Phillips said, "No further questions."

Judge Moorman said, "Mr. Mason."

Mason studied the witness for a moment and then spoke: "Lieutenant Latham, you have testified that when you arrived at the Adrian house, you observed Laurel Adrian walking away from the front door of the house, is that correct?"

"That is correct."

"So, you assume from that that she had been in the house prior to—"

"Objection, Your Honor." D.A. Phillips was on his feet. "Mr. Mason is asking the witness for an assumption."

Judge Moorman said, "I'll sustain. Proceed, Mr. Mason."

Mason walked toward the witness stand, and reframed his question.

"Lieutenant Latham, you testified that you saw Laurel Adrian walking away from the front door of the house—"

"—Yes—"

"—And do you have proof that she had been in the house just prior to your arrival?"

"No, sir."

"No proof at all?"

"No, sir."

"All right." Mason stood directly in front of the witness stand. "And didn't Laurel Adrian tell you she had arrived at the house at almost exactly the same time you did? And didn't she tell you where she had been earlier?"

Phillips stood again. "Objection! The witness has already testified—"

"Overruled, Mr. Phillips," Judge Moorman said. "Mr. Mason has the right to question the testimony if he plans to lead us to some different conclusion than the witness implied. Let's wait and see."

"Thank you, Your Honor," Mason made a small bow and turned back to Lieutenant Latham.

"Did you, did the police, make any effort to try to disprove Laurel Adrian's statement to you? That she had been on her way to the beach house and that she had phoned her house in the hills from along the way before she returned?"

Lieutenant Latham appeared bewildered.

"No, sir. I have no knowledge that any such effort was made."

Phillips was standing again. Mason half turned to glance at him as if inviting an objection. Phillips sat down.

Mason returned to his cross-examination.

"For instance, Lieutenant, when Laurel Adrian told you she had phoned the house from a pay phone along the way, as you have testified, did it ever occur to you to make a check of the calls made from that pay phone to see if she was telling the truth?"

The lieutenant swallowed hard.

"No, no, it didn't occur to me, sir."

Mason said, "Did you ever think to ask her the location of the pay phone? Did anyone bother to ask her?"

"Not to my knowledge, no, sir."

"I see. It really wouldn't have been that difficult to have checked the phone."

Mason started slowly back toward the defense table.

"Objection!" Phillips called out. "Mr. Mason is expressing an opinion."

Mason half turned and looked at Latham and, as if he had only paused, asked, "Would it, Lieutenant?"

"No, I guess it wouldn't have been that difficult," Latham answered.

Mason nodded to Phillips. Phillips was still standing. Mason sat down at the defense table.

Judge Moorman, covering a smile with his hand, nodded to Carter Phillips.

"Does the prosecution want to reexamine?"

"Yes, Your Honor."

The D.A. had a file in his hand. He glanced at the file and looked up at Lieutenant Latham.

"Lieutenant, I see here in a copy of the statement Laurel Adrian gave you that she told you when she called her house there was no answer. Is that correct?"

"Yeah—yes, sir," Latham said, suddenly recalling the statement. He nodded his head. "That's right, that's what she said."

"So you knew if you tried to trace the call from the pay phone, there couldn't be a record if the call was not completed, correct?"

Latham was smiling broadly.

"Yes, sir. There couldn't have been a record if the call wasn't completed."

"No further questions," Phillips said, clearly pleased with himself.

Mason was on his feet, hand upraised.

The judge said, "I take it you have another question of this witness, Mr. Mason."

"I do, Your Honor."

"Proceed."

Mason said, "Lieutenant Latham, you and the other officers at the murder scene that night certainly must have carefully observed the den and everything in it."

Latham was frowning.

"Yes, sir."

Mason picked up a copy of the photograph of the den that the D.A. had entered into the record. He held up the photograph.

"And equally certainly, you had ample time to study this photograph of the den?"

"Yes."

"Then, I put it to you: On the desk, in the den, as you can clearly see in this photograph, the telephone is attached to an answering machine. You see that?"

Mason had walked to the witness stand and handed the photograph to Latham.

"I see, yes."

"Which means," Mason said, his voice stern, "if Laurel Adrian's call from the pay phone had been traced, even though no one answered, the call would have been completed, and there would have been a record."

Mason walked away from the witness stand. Out of the corner of his eye he could see that Carter Phillips was slumped down in his chair.

Mason said, "I have no further questions, Your Honor."

"Oh, you were good, Mr. Mason," Laurel whispered as he sat down next to her. Mason leaned toward her.

"When I was a kid, on the Fourth of July, the kids in the neighborhood would toss little cherry bombs to explode on the sidewalk around the feet of the other little kids, which made them jump." He grinned. "That's what I've been doing so far today. The cherry bombs didn't exactly do any real damage but they sure kept you hopping and off-balance."

Carter Phillips called his next witness, Dr. James Lee, chief medical examiner for Los Angeles County. He was a solemn man, tall, thin, bald-headed, in his sixties.

He tesitfied that he had performed the autopsy on the body of Gilbert Adrian.

"And what were your findings, Doctor?" Phillips asked.

The medical examiner held up a file folder.

"The complete autopsy report is here."

Phillips nodded. "We will enter it into the record, but for now could you give us the conclusions in your own words?"

Carter Phillips paused while the judge looked at Perry Mason, who stood.

"The defense has no objections."

The judge nodded to Dr. Lee, who said, "There were two

bullet wounds in the skull, in the cerebrum area—to be precise, in the frontal lobe, sometimes called the 'motor lobe.' Both internal wounds in the frontal lobe corresponded to the exterior wounds at the entrance to the trajectory the bullets followed; that is, matched the external wounds in the center of the forehead and between the eyes."

"And based on your autopsy, you were able to determine the cause of death?"

"Yes." The medical examiner nodded. "Either of the cerebrum wounds was sufficient to have caused instantaneous death and, in tandem, both did."

Phillips nodded gravely. "And did the bullets exit the skull?"

"No. Both bullets remained inside the cranium. Both bullets were recovered and handed over to ballistics for possible identification."

"Now, Doctor, what time was it, as exactly as possible, when the victim expired?"

"Between ten and ten-thirty P.M."

"You are certain about that?"

"Positive. The time of death can be fixed to have occurred during that thirty-minute period."

"Thank you, Doctor."

Mason rose briefly to say, "The defense reserves the right to question this witness at a later time."

He glanced at the autopsy report while Phillips called as his next witness the police photographer who had taken pictures of Gil Adrian's body at the murder scene and later, stripped, at the morgue.

Mason had no objections when the photographs were entered into the record and no questions to be asked of the photographer.

A member of the police forensic unit was the next witness to take the stand. He testified that Gil Adrian's den, the .38 revolver and the .32 revolver found at the scene had been dusted for latent fingerprints.

"In the den the only prints that could be identified belonged either to the victim, Gilbert Adrian, the defendant, Mrs. Adrian, or to the first officers at the scene, the lieutenant and two of his men."

"And the thirty-eight revolver?"

"It had been wiped clean."

"How about the thirty-two revolver?"

"It, too, had been wiped clean."

"Tell me," Carter Phillips asked, "how many fingerprints do you do a year?"

"I do forty-five thousand a year."

"Thank you." The D.A. turned toward the defense table. "No further questions."

Mason, on his feet, asked, "Isn't it true that most weapons examined by you, which have been left behind at a homicide scene, are wiped clean of all prints?"

"That's frequently the case, yes."

"So that no matter who wielded the murder weapon, it wouldn't be particularly significant to find that the prints would have been wiped away?"

"Not particularly significant, no, sir."

Mason nodded and asked, "Sir, did you find *evidence* of any other fingerprints in the den?"

"Yes, sir. A few. Partial prints that could have belonged to either or both of the Adrians or to another party or parties. It was impossible to determine."

"Thank you. No further questions."

Mason made a couple of notations on his yellow pad while the next prosecution witness took the stand and was sworn in. Ernest Boyer was the forensic unit's ballistics expert.

Boyer identified the two bullets recovered from Gil Adrian's skull as having been fired from the .32 revolver.

With that fact established, Carter Phillips proceeded to ask, "I believe you also examined the two bullets removed from the body of the man who called himself"—the D.A. glanced at the pages he had in his hand—"Karl Braundorff, who was shot by Gilbert Adrian at the Oaks—"

"Objection, Your Honor! Objection!" Mason's voice rang out loud, startling the judge and Carter Phillips.

Judge Moorman stared out at Perry Mason.

"Objection, Your Honor. We have had testimony but no evidence, no proof, that this man, Karl Braundorff, is in fact dead. I submit that there is no proof of record—"

Carter Phillips shook his head in exasperation.

Judge Moorman beckoned with his hand for both men to approach the bench.

"Now, Mr. Phillips," the judge said quizzically to the D.A., "what say you to Mr. Mason's objection?"

"I'd say, Your Honor," Phillips replied, annoyed, "that Mr. Mason knows perfectly well that the death of the man Adrian shot has no bearing on this case except insofar as the time element between his death and Adrian's own is concerned. Which is what I'm trying to develop."

The judge looked at Mason.

Mason said, "I don't see how evidence can be allowed about possible bullets removed from the body of some corpse when we've been offered no proof, only unverified testimony, that there was a corpse in the first place."

The D.A. glared at Mason. "You mean you want the medical examiner recalled to the stand to present such testimony?"

"That would seem the most likely way to do it," Mason said reasonably.

"Your objection is sustained, Mr. Mason," Judge Moorman said. He looked at the D.A. "Mr. Phillips, you will recall the medical examiner."

"But, Your Honor," Phillips sputtered, "Dr. Lee has left the courtroom. I doubt that I can get him back today."

"In that case," the judge said, "we will adjourn until tomorrow morning. You will produce the medical examiner, Mr. Phillips."

Perry Mason quickly gathered up his notes and briefcase and, taking Laurel by the arm, hurried toward the rear doors.

The TV cameras and reporters were gathered on the sidewalk outside the courthouse, crowding around Carter Phillips until they spotted Mason and Laurel.

Suddenly the D.A. was left alone as the newsmen rushed toward Mason and his client, shouting a barrage of questions.

Laurel shrank back. Mason, smiling affably at the cameras, tried to reassure her with the pressure of his hand on her arm, and deflected attention from her to himself by addressing the group.

"As the prosecution so amply demonstrated today, this is a case built solely on the shaky foundation of circumstantial evidence. All we have heard so far is testimony of coincidences and happenstances which will not withstand the scrutiny of any fair-minded jury if we go to trial, I am certain."

At the beginning of the hearing Mason had arranged for a car and driver to transport Laurel to and from court each day. Out of the corner of his eye he saw Della Street signaling from the curb where the car was waiting.

"You will excuse us now, please," he said to the newsmen and led Laurel quickly across the sidewalk and into the car.

Della, who had been holding the rear car door open, followed Laurel, and Mason eased inside and closed the door. The TV cameras and reporters had trailed after them to the car. Mason, still smiling affably, gave them a wave of his hand.

As the car pulled away, Mason spotted Carter Phillips trudging along the sidewalk, briefcase in hand, shoulders hunched as if he were carrying the weight of the world.

Mason reflected, with some satisfaction, that at least he was making the D.A. work for the pay he earned from the taxpayers' dollars.

17

As the hearing reconvened the next morning, Dr. James Lee, the medical examiner, returned to the witness stand.

After Judge Moorman reminded him that he was still under oath, Dr. Lee testified to the autopsy he had performed on the man who called himself Karl Braundorff.

Carter Phillips's questions were terse, the medical examiner's answers brief.

The autopsy had revealed the body contained two bullet wounds, one in the head, one in the chest. The bullet wound in the chest was the cause of death, having penetrated the downward apex of the heart, the bullet coming to rest inside the chest cavity against the fifth rib. This bullet was recovered from the chest as was the bullet from the head. Both bullets were sent on to ballistics. The time of death was established as between nine-thirty and ten P.M.

The D.A. asked that the autopsy report be entered into the record.

Mason had no objection. And he again reserved the right to question the medical examiner at a later time.

Dr. Lee stepped down and Carter Phillips called Ernest Boyer, the forensic unit's ballistic's expert, to resume the testimony that had been interrupted by Mason's objection the previous day.

"You have previously identified the two bullets recovered from Gilbert Adrian's skull as having been fired from the thirty-two-caliber revolver, marked People's Exhibit Three-A, is that correct?"

"That is correct."

Phillips nodded. "To take up now where we left off yesterday, did you examine the two bullets recovered from the body of a man who called himself Karl Braundorff?"

"I did."

"And what were your conclusions?"

"I found that the two bullets removed from his body were fired from the thirty-eight revolver, the weapon found on the desk."

"I now ask you to examine the thirty-two-caliber revolver, the revolver registered to Mrs. Laurel Adrian."

Boyer looked carefully at the tag attached to the revolver handed to him by the D.A.

Boyer nodded. "This is the gun, the same gun that fired the two shots that killed Gilbert Adrian. My marking is on the tag."

"Your witness, Mr. Mason," Carter Phillips said.

"Isn't it true there were two bullet holes found in the wall behind the desk in the Adrian den?" Mason asked Ernest Boyer.

"Yes, sir, there were."

"Did you personally remove the two bullets from the wall?"

"I did, yes, sir. And I examined them."

"You examined them. And what did you find?"

"Both bullets had been fired from the thirty-eight revolver."

"The revolver used to kill the man at the Oaks Restaurant?" Mason asked.

"Yes, sir."

"The revolver found on Gilbert Adrian's desk at the time the police entered the house?"

Boyer nodded.

Mason nodded. He asked, "And before you removed the bullets from the wall, did you carefully examine the holes themselves? To judge the trajectory of the shots?"

"Yes, sir, I did."

"And what did you find?"

Boyer answered, "The bullets had been fired directly into the wall, straight into it."

"Not at an angle?" Mason asked. "You're certain of that?"

"I'm certain, yes, sir."

"And did you measure the distance from the floor of the two holes in the wall where the bullets were lodged?"

Boyer nodded. "The distance was six feet two inches."

"Yes," Mason agreed, "it was." He looked toward the judge. "Your Honor, the defense would now like to introduce Exhibit A."

Judge Moorman nodded. "Proceed, Mr. Mason."

Mason turned and looked toward the rear of the courtroom, and made a motion with his hand.

Drake and a man in white coveralls came forward carrying between them a large plyboard partition. High up on the plywood partition were two holes. When Drake and the other man were alongside the defense table, they stopped, holding the partition upright between them.

Mason looked at Ernest Boyer. "Would the witness please step down and approach the exhibit."

Ernest Boyer walked over to where Drake stood with the man in the overalls. Mason joined Boyer, handing him a tape measure and asking, "Would you now measure the distance from the floor to the two holes on the exhibit?"

Boyer took the measurement, looked at Mason, and said, "Exactly six feet two inches."

Mason nodded. "Precisely the height of the two bullet holes in the wall of Gilbert Adrian's den, is that correct?"

"That is correct."

"And you have testified that the shots entered the wall directly, straight on, that is, and not at an angle."

"That was my finding," Boyer agreed.

Mason asked, "Would you tell us now, as an expert witness, your opinion of the height of the person who fired the shots?"

Boyer frowned. "I would say that whoever fired the shots would have to have been at least five feet ten inches tall, perhaps more."

"But not less?" Mason asked.

"In my opinion, no."

"In your expert opinion?"

"All right. Yes, sir."

Mason put a finger on the white square and said, "This is five feet ten inches." With his other hand, Mason gestured to Laurel and she stood. It was clearly apparent that she was several inches shorter than the five-feet-ten-inch-high spot to which Mason was pointing.

Mason nodded to Laurel and she sat down. He said to Boyer, "Would you please take the stand again."

Drake and the other man carried the partition toward the back of the courtroom. Ernest Boyer returned to the witness stand.

Mason went back to the defense table and looked at his notes, then said, "As the ballistics expert, were you asked to make an examination of another gun, as well, in connection with the deaths of Gilbert Adrian and of Karl Braundorff?"

"I was."

"A twenty-two-caliber pistol, recovered from the body of Karl Braundorff?"

"A twenty-two-caliber pistol, yes," Boyer agreed. "I was told, but have no personal knowledge, that it was in the possession of Karl Braundorff at the time of his death."

"And what were you looking for in your examination of the pistol?"

"Whether or not the weapon had been fired recently."

"And had it?"

"No, sir."

"No further questions."

Mason sat down. There was a brief delay while Carter Phillips conferred with one of his assistants.

Mason noted that Della Street had been visibly annoyed during his cross-examination of Boyer, and it had nothing to do with the legal proceedings going on in the courtroom. Her annoyance came from the fact that she had noticed that one of the sketch artists who worked for a television network was apparently doing a drawing of Mason from her place at the press table.

Della had recognized the woman artist, who had all her attention focused on Mason, and guessed her sketch of him would be shown on the TV news later that day or evening. Della had seen many of the artist's trial sketches on television and thought them to be more like slipshod caricatures than semblances of their subjects, mostly done with broad lines and smudges so that the supposed likenesses, male and female, appeared to be bearded. Della always complained about the sketches and Mason found her irritation amusing.

Mason turned his attention toward Lieutenant Ray Dallas, the next witness to be called by Phillips, as the D.A. asked:

"Lieutenant Dallas, I believe you were placed in charge of the investigation of Mrs. Laurel Adrian at the time she was brought into the station house on the night of her husband's murder?"

"I was."

"And you interrogated her that night?"

"I did."

"You have read the testimony given in this court by Lieutenant Frank Latham?"

"I have. I've read it carefully."

"Now, based upon your own interrogation of the defendant, is there anything you would add to, or subtract from, his account of the answers the defendant gave him."

"No, sir."

"She gave you the same answers, in all respects?"

"In all respects. Exactly the same answers. In fact, in most instances, word for word."

"Objection!" Mason was on his feet, shaking his head. "The phrase 'word for word' is too imprecise. If the witness means to imply 'word for word' literally, I ask that evidence be produced of every word Laurel Adrian gave in response to questions by Lieutenant Latham and every word she gave in response to questions by Lieutenant Dallas."

"Objection sustained." Judge Moorman looked from Mason to Phillips.

Phillips nodded. "I will rephrase the question." He turned toward Dallas.

"Lieutenant, were the answers the defendant gave to Lieutenant Latham the same answers she gave to you, in all respects?"

"In all respects, yes, sir."

"All right. Now, moving on, subsequent to the night of the

murder, did you attempt to verify the movements of Gilbert Adrian on the day of his death?"

"I did."

"And were you successful?"

"I was." Dallas nodded.

"And would you tell the court the results of your findings."

Dallas referred to a sheet of paper he held in his hand.

"Nine A.M. to five P.M. the above date—Gilbert Adrian in his office, testified to by two sources: Megan Calder, secretary to Gilbert Adrian, and Kay Milner, receptionist, both at Adrian Enterprises, Incorporated."

Dallas glanced up and then back at the sheet of paper.

"Five-fifteen P.M. to eight-thirty P.M.—Gilbert Adrian in a meeting with Jerome Dayton at the C.P.A. offices of Kenyon, West, and Silverton, testified to by two sources: Jerome Dayton, Gilbert Adrian's personal accountant, and Elizabeth Parkhurst, secretary to Jerome Dayton. Nine P.M. to nine-forty-five P.M.— Gilbert Adrian at the Oaks Restaurant, testified to by John Fallon, manager, and Edward Deegan, bartender, Oaks Restaurant. Ten-thirty P.M.—Gilbert Adrian found dead in the den of his house, testified to by Lieutenant Frank Latham and Sergeant Samuel Fisher, Los Angeles Police Department."

"And did you yourself inspect the scene of the crime on the night of Gilbert Adrian's murder?"

"I did."

"You have seen photographs taken of Gilbert Adrian's den that night, photographs now entered into the records of this court?"

"I have."

"Do the photographs accurately picture the disarray of the room?"

"They do."

The D.A. walked closer to the witness stand as he asked, "In the only time that day that Gilbert Adrian *could* conceivably have been in that room, would it have been possible, in such a brief time as it was, for him to have created such disarray?"

Perry Mason stood. "Objection! Speculative, calls for an opinion on the part of the witness."

Judge Moorman said, with a passing smile, "Mr. Mason, despite the convoluted phrasing of the prosecutor's question, almost to the point of obscurity, I'm going to overrule. The witness may answer."

"No, sir," Lieutenant Dallas said, "it would not have been possible."

"Your witness," Phillips said, nodding to Perry Mason.

Mason, who was still standing, said, "Lieutenant, we have had testimony about this man who called himself Karl Braundorff but whose true identity seems to remain unknown to the police until this day, correct?"

"Yes."

"And did you see his body the night of his murder?"

"I did."

Mason nodded. "There has also been testimony that he had a twenty-two pistol on his person at that time. Is *that* correct?"

"Yes."

"And where was this weapon concealed on his person?"

"In an ankle holster."

"In an ankle holster," Mason repeated thoughtfully. "Curious."

Mason rubbed his forehead for a moment. "And you still haven't been able to find out who this man was?"

"No, sir. As I have already testified."

"But you have made efforts?"

Dallas nodded. "We have. But if, as seems possible, the man was an alien—in this country illegally—it wouldn't be all that unusual that he has not yet been identified. There are such instances in police files everywhere across the nation."

Mason's next question was delivered in an offhand manner: "And as part of your efforts, did you ever question Gilbert Adrian's personal bodyguard, Steven Benedict?"

Dallas stared at Mason blankly, started to speak, and changed his mind. He looked toward Carter Phillips for help.

The D.A. stood up slowly. "Your Honor, may we approach the bench?"

Judge Moorman nodded. Mason and Phillips came forward. "Now what is all this?"

"Your Honor," Carter Phillips, highly agitated, said, "it would appear that Mr. Mason has been improperly withholding vital evidence in this case. The state has no knowledge that Gilbert Adrian had a personal bodyguard."

The judge looked at Mason.

"Counselor?"

"And I had no knowledge that the state didn't discover that Gilbert Adrian had a personal bodyguard. I did. And I shall be only too willing to provide Mr. Phillips with the man's name, address, and phone number."

Mason handed the information on a sheet of paper to the D.A.

"Do you think now with Mr. Mason's help you will be able to locate this person, Mr. Phillips?" the judge inquired dryly.

"Yes, Your Honor. But I'll have to ask for a continuance."

"Agreed," Judge Moorman said.

Mason went back to the defense table while the judge was announcing his ruling to the court.

Mason noticed that Lieutenant Ray Dallas had stepped down from the witness stand and was conferring with Carter Phillips.

The whole courtroom had been taken by surprise by the sudden suspension of the proceedings.

Mason beckoned to Della and said, "I don't think you'll have too much trouble getting Laurel out to the car if you go now. Don't talk to the reporters."

He turned to Laurel. "I'll see you tonight at dinner."

"Oh, yes," she said. "I hadn't forgotten."

Mason watched them walk away and then began gathering his notes and papers together. He saw Ray Dallas approaching as he had suspected would happen; this was the reason he had delayed his departure.

"Well, sir," Dallas said, half smiling, "you kind of shook up the prosecution, and at least this member of the police department, with your revelation that Adrian employed a bodyguard. I sure slipped up at not uncovering that one."

"I'm sorry, Ray," Mason said. "I didn't enjoy making you look bad on the witness stand." He rubbed his forehead with a finger. "It was just dumb luck that I found out about him. And I *did* try to get the information to you. As soon as I discovered him, I stopped by your office several times and phoned you. You were never in, or so they told me. I guess you didn't get my messages."

Dallas shook his head. "You know I got your messages. I wouldn't mislead you about that."

"But you didn't get back to me."

"It's all Carter Phillips's fault. Somebody told him they'd seen us together at lunch. He didn't like the idea of us being chummy. He spoke to the police commissioner and I got orders from above to avoid you until this hearing was over."

"I'll tell you the truth, Ray. I figured that might have happened."

As they left the courtroom, Dallas glanced sideways curiously at Mason. "You know, Perry, there's one thing I've been wondering about ever since you sprang this surprise on us."

"What's that?"

"I've been wondering, since you were pretty certain we didn't know about this fellow, why didn't you wait and spring him on the prosecution as a surprise witness of your own?"

"I guess I could have done it that way."

Dallas said, "Of course, it could be you talked to the guy and found out that Gil Adrian never mentioned to him, the bodyguard, that your client might pose a possible threat to him."

Mason said nothing.

"In that case," Dallas said, "it would be better for you to have the prosecution call him to testify. Something Carter Phillips will have to do, now that the judge knows about this guy, and must be curious, too."

Mason grinned. "That sounds like it would have been a devious thing for me to have done."

"Or good courtroom tactics," Dallas said.

"Sounds better that way." Mason grinned again.

18

Laurel was already waiting at the table Mason had reserved at the restaurant when he arrived.

They ordered wine and dinner and she said, "I saw your picture on television just before I left the house. They were doing a story on the news about today's hearing. Actually, it wasn't a picture of you. It was one of those artist's sketches. It didn't really look like you."

Mason grinned. "Those sketches drive Della to distraction. I hope she didn't see the newscast." He raised his eyebrows. "Incidentally, I thought I suggested to you that you not watch the news of the trial on television."

"I haven't really. Not that much. I just happened to see it today," she said, looking at him innocently.

Mason realized they were only making small talk and he nodded and waited for Laurel to ask him the questions he was certain she must have on her mind.

Laurel took a sip of wine and said, "Mr. Mason, I can take the truth. How do you think we're doing so far?"

"The truth?" He said without pausing, "So far as I see it, they have a serious problem and we have a serious problem."

"Please go on."

"Their problem is establishing a motive strong enough to over-come reasonable doubt. Although, make no mistake about it, the D.A. is going to present an assortment of motives, hoping he can make one of them persuasive enough to influence the judge."

She shook her head dismally. "And that's going to be a problem for *him*?"

"Sure. Most of them I think we'll be able to answer. The prose-cution would be on stronger ground if they had a single powerful motive that would hold up against reasonable doubt."

He looked at her gravely. "Our serious problem is the time element. How to explain how everything that happened could have transpired between the time your husband left the restau-rant and was found shot to death. Frankly, I haven't even come close to sorting that one out."

He shook his head impatiently. "I can show that there were people who had reason to go gunning for your husband. But"—he shook his head again impatiently—"I can't *prove* any of them had anything to do with his murder. It's a tangled skein I haven't yet been able to unravel. My hunch is that all the various pieces fit together and once I can figure them out, I can prove your inno-cence."

"I wish I could help you more," Laurel said.

When their dinners were served, Mason said, "Laurel, you've never mentioned any family or friends. Don't you have anyone close to you?"

"As far as my family goes," she said, "I was an only child. My parents were drowned in a boating accident off Catalina Island about five years ago. I have one uncle, my father's brother, who lives in Paris. He phones me every once in a long while. We were never close but he wanted to bring his wife over to be with me after Gil's death. I didn't see any point in it. And besides, why should they have to be subjected to such an unpleasant experi-ence?"

"And friends?"

"They all drifted out of my life after I married Gil," she said simply. "Or maybe I drifted out of their lives. Gil was the kind of man who demanded all my time. Or at least he did for a while."

She looked off into the distance and then back at Mason. "You know, you've never questioned me about how I came to marry a man like Gil Adrian, I mean like the man he turned out to be."

"I didn't believe it was any of my business, as far as defending you was concerned, nor important as far as the trial was concerned."

"Still—you must have wondered."

"All right." Mason smiled. "I guess I have. But I thought if it was something you wanted to tell me, you would."

Laurel said slowly, "When I first met Gil, he was unlike anyone I had ever encountered before in my life. He was so confident, so dynamic, in the way he moved through the world, as if he could accomplish anything he set out to do. Being with him, married to him, he made me feel the same way about myself."

She took a sip of coffee and Mason waited, wanting her to continue to talk.

"The first time we met," she said, "he came into the little antique shop I'd started with the money my parents had left me. He was there looking for articles to furnish some of the offices at Adrian Enterprises. He bought everything in the shop, and then invited me to go out for dinner."

She frowned a little. "Those were the good moments. He had such charm he made you believe whatever he thought or wanted or did was right. He had the same effect on almost everyone. I saw it in other people around him. Lately, I've often wondered how I could have been so misled."

Mason said kindly, "I can understand, Laurel. I can believe that everything you've said of him seemed to be true, and therefore reason enough for you to have married him."

"Do you mean that?"

"I do. Absolutely. And I'm glad you told me."

She smiled for the first time since she had started to explain her feelings about Adrian. "I'm glad, too."

They finished dinner and Mason escorted her out to the car and chauffeur waiting to drive her home.

Earlier Mason had made a date to meet Drake. He had started to walk the few blocks to the Brent Building where their offices were located when he heard his name being called.

It was Drake waiting in a car at the curb. Drake motioned urgently and Mason hurried over and got into the car.

Drake pulled out from the curb and sped rapidly down the street.

"What's up, Paul?"

"Somebody new's tailing our client," Drake said, "and it's not the police this time."

"How do you know?"

Drake kept his eyes on the road as he drove. "When I came out of the courthouse today, after you and Della and Laurel Adrian got into the car, I spotted this character I know parked across the street. I saw him drive off, following you. I got into my car and followed him. He's been tailing our client all day right up to now and I've been tailing him."

"Who is he?"

"He's a private investigator. Name's Charley Dumas. A sleazy operator, specializes in trying to turn up dirt for clients out to get somebody. The kind of guy who gives my business a bad name."

Mason was frowning. "And he's been watching Laurel all day?"

Drake nodded. "After she got home from court, she went out shopping and he followed her, followed her home again, and followed her when she came to meet you in the restaurant. You probably didn't notice but he even went inside the restaurant while you were both there, I guess to check out who she was meeting."

"He doesn't know you're onto him?"

"Nope. I wonder who hired him?"

Mason said, "And what's he looking for?"

Drake was silent for a moment before he said, "Perry, are you sure this dame's innocent?"

"Until proven guilty."

Both men were quiet on the rest of the drive out to Laurel Adrian's beach house.

Drake parked well back on the road from the car that had been following Laurel.

They watched when she went into the house and the limousine that had taken her to the restaurant and home again drove off.

They could see that the private investigator, Charley Dumas, was still parked up nearer to the house.

After a while all the lights in the house went out and a few minutes later Charley Dumas drove away.

"Let him go," Mason said. "Let's head back to L.A. But starting tomorrow morning, I want you to put a tail on Dumas. Rotate your operatives. I want to know when he's following Laurel, and where *he* goes and whom he sees. We'll give him a dose of his own medicine."

19

The first thing Perry Mason noticed when the hearing resumed the next morning was that Steven Benedict was in court and would presumably be called as a witness by the prosecution.

Ray Dallas was on the witness stand as he had been the previous day when Mason's question to him in cross-examination had brought on the abrupt recess of the proceedings.

Judge Moorman leaned forward and said, "The clerk will now read back the last question Mr. Mason put to this witness yesterday."

The clerk stood and read: "Question: And as part of your efforts, did you ever question Gilbert Adrian's personal bodyguard, Steven Benedict?"

"Thank you," Judge Moorman said. He looked at Dallas. "The witness will now answer."

Dallas looked at Mason, who was standing directly in front of him, and said, "Yes, yes, I have questioned Steven Benedict."

"Your Honor," Carter Phillips interjected, "Steven Benedict is here in court and will be the next witness to testify. If Mr. Mason will concur, it will save time if we reserve all questions concerning him until he takes the witness stand."

"I concur," Mason said, nodding to the judge and to the D.A.

"Thank you, Counselor." Phillips sat down.

Mason walked away. "No further questions."

Phillips, who had expected Mason to continue his cross-examination, was slow getting to his feet. "The state calls Steven Benedict."

Mason watched Benedict come forward to the witness stand, Benedict standing stiffly at attention as he was sworn in.

Mason leaned close to Laurel. "You're certain you never saw this man before?"

"I really don't think so, Mr. Mason."

"He says he's seen you with your husband, sometimes, at the office."

"That's possible," Laurel said. "I used to visit the office on a few occasions, to pick up Gil after work or if he had an errand he wanted me to run for him. I told you this man looked familiar to me. Maybe that's when I saw him without really noticing."

Carter Phillips had begun his examination of Steven Benedict.

"You were employed by the deceased, Gilbert Adrian, is that correct?"

"Yes."

"In what capacity, what was your job?"

"I was hired by him to be his bodyguard."

"And for what period of time did you perform these services?"

"For six months. That is, for six months until he was killed."

"Did he ever tell you why he needed a bodyguard?"

"No, not exactly."

Phillips frowned. "Not exactly? I don't understand."

"What he said when he hired me was he wanted somebody around to keep an eye on things, in case there ever was any trouble."

"And was there ever any trouble?"

"Well," Benedict said slowly, "a couple of times when he was out in public there would be people come up to him, want to ask him favors, things like that. He would sort of nod to me, times like that, and I would get rid of them."

"I see." Phillips thought for a moment. "But you did carry a gun, didn't you?"

"Yes, sir. I'm licensed."

"And Mr. Adrian knew you carried a gun, didn't he?"

"He knew." Benedict nodded.

"In fact, he wanted you to be armed."

"Carrying a gun was part of my job."

"Now we come to the night of May eleventh," Phillips said. "Did Mr. Adrian tell you where he was going that night? Did he tell you who he was meeting?"

"Not before he went, no, sir, he didn't tell me where he was going."

"Not before he went, he didn't tell you?" The D.A.'s voice was puzzled. "Then, are you saying he did tell you but not before?"

"Yes."

"When? When did he tell you?"

"He phoned me from the Oaks Restaurant that night. He said he was there. He didn't tell me who he was meeting. He just wanted to tell me I could have the next day off."

"If he was meeting someone he feared, wouldn't he have wanted you there?"

"Objection!" Mason was standing. "Calls for speculation on the part of the witness."

"Objection sustained."

"Mr. Benedict," Phillips said, "was there ever an occasion while you were employed by Mr. Adrian that he revealed to you that he did fear for his life?"

Benedict leaned far forward in his chair. "Yes, sir, there was."

"Would you tell the court, please."

"It was around the first of May. He told me somebody took a shot at him at his beach house one night. He told me about it the next morning. He said he was just coming out of his house to get into his car and somebody fired a bullet at him in the darkness. He couldn't see who it was and then he heard a car driving away. He tried to follow in his car but all four of his tires had been slashed."

"And he didn't tell you if he thought he knew who it was?"

"No." Benedict shook his head.

"Did he make a report to the police?"

"I asked him that, too. He said, no, he wasn't going to because he didn't want any publicity about it."

Carter Phillips stood for a moment in indecision and finally said, "Your witness, Mr. Mason."

Mason walked to the front of the courtroom. "Tell me, Mr. Benedict, how did you come to be employed by Mr. Adrian?"

"I answered a newspaper ad Mr. Adrian had run."

"A newspaper ad? Did it say 'personal bodyguard' wanted?"

Benedict smiled. "No, sir. The ad said someone was wanted for security work. That's my line of work so I answered."

"And he hired you?"

"He interviewed me," Benedict said, "and checked my references and credentials, and hired me."

"And how were you paid?"

"I was paid by the company, Mr. Adrian's company."

"I see," Mason said. "And how were you carried on the company payroll?"

Benedict said, "As I think I told you before, I was carried as a part of the company's security staff."

"Yes. All a somewhat informal arrangement, wasn't it?"

"I guess you could say so. I don't know. I figured that's the way he wanted to do it, so—" Benedict shrugged.

"So, actually, you were just part of the security staff—"

"Your Honor! Objection!" Phillips said, "Immaterial. Counsel is fishing—"

"Your Honor," Mason said. "I'm trying to establish that Mr. Benedict's employment by Gilbert Adrian as a personal bodyguard was a somewhat vague arrangement and not necessarily because the deceased really feared for his life."

"If that's a valid point, I don't think you're going to be able to elicit any more information on it from this witness," Judge Moorman said. "Objection sustained. Move on, Mr. Mason."

Mason turned and paced back and forth in front of the witness stand. "Mr. Benedict, you have testified to the prosecutor that Mr. Adrian never told you why he needed a bodyguard, didn't you?"

"Yes, sir. He never did."

"Never mentioned anyone he thought might be a danger to him?"

"No. He never did."

Mason stopped his pacing and stood directly in front of the witness stand. "He never, in word or action, indicated to you that the defendant, his wife, Laurel Adrian, sitting there, was a threat to his life?"

"No." Benedict took a deep breath. "I have to say he never did."

"That's all, Mr. Benedict. Thank you."

Carter Phillips had no further questions. Steven Benedict stepped down from the witness stand.

"Mr. Phillips," the judge said, "call your next witness."

At the defense table, Laurel Adrian clutched Perry Mason's arm as Randolph Adrian came forward and was sworn in.

Phillips asked, "Mr. Randolph Adrian, what was your relationship to the victim, Gilbert Adrian?"

"He was my father."

"Which makes the defendant, Laurel Adrian—?"

"My stepmother."

"Now do you have any information that might be pertinent to this case of what your father, Gilbert Adrian, planned to do on the day after he was murdered?"

"I do," Randolph Adrian answered, his voice rising. "He planned to change his will, cutting my stepmother, his wife, Laurel Adrian, out of any inheritance."

"He told you this?"

"He did."

"And was anyone else present at the time he told you?"

"No." Randolph Adrian shot a look at Laurel. "But after he told me, I was in his office when he phoned his lawyer, William Catlin, and made the appointment to talk to him about changing the will."

"That would have been on the day of May eleventh, when your father phoned his lawyer?"

"May eleventh, that's when it was. And the night before that date was to be kept, my father was murdered."

"You're certain," Phillips said, "that it was his intention to cut her, the defendant, out of his will?"

"Absolutely! They were going to divorce. I suppose the settlement he was going to have to make—"

"Objection!"

"Sustained."

Phillips said, "Mr. Adrian, thank you." He turned, offering the witness to Mason.

Mason gave Laurel a reassuring pat on the arm before he stood.

"Now, Mr. Adrian, isn't it true that if your father's will *had* been changed, you have reason to believe that you would have inherited?"

"Yes." Randolph Adrian nodded his head. "He told me that was his intention."

"Consequently, you have good cause to feel resentment, anger, that the will was not changed?"

"Yes, I suppose you could say that. But that has nothing to do—"

Mason glanced at the judge. "Your Honor?"

Judge Moorman made a motion toward Randolph Adrian. "The witness will confine his answers to the questions asked by counsel."

"Mr. Adrian, do you have any knowledge, any knowledge whatsoever, that your stepmother knew of your father's plans to change his will?"

"I guess not, no," Adrian admitted.

"Do you have any knowledge, any knowledge whatsoever, that Laurel Adrian knew that your father planned to meet with his lawyer on the date you have stated?"

"No."

"So, despite your testimony here, the one action may have no connection with the other, is that not correct? Only a coincidence?"

Mason didn't expect an answer. He stepped back. "My cross-examination of this witness is concluded."

"The people call Angela Ryerson," Carter Phillips announced.

Laurel whispered a question to Mason, "Is she that baby-sitter you mentioned to me?"

Mason nodded. "She's the one, Angie Ryerson."

The sixteen-year-old had a pretty face and auburn hair tied with a pink bow to match the color of her linen dress and short-sleeved jacket.

Laurel shook her head. "I don't ever in my life remember seeing her."

Under questioning by Carter Phillips, Angie Ryerson related that she had been baby-sitting for the Hendrens family, who lived on the corner of the street where the Adrian house was located. Mr. and Mrs. Hendrens had gone shopping for two hours and had arrived home at eight P.M. on the night of May 11.

"You're certain of the time?" the D.A. asked.

"Yes, sir. I'm paid by the hour so I know exactly what time it was," she answered, getting a smile from the judge and most of the people in the courtroom.

She said she left the Hendrens house to walk home, a block and a half away. As she passed the Adrian house, she saw a car come along the street and turn into a driveway.

"And did you recognize who the car belonged to?"

"Yes. It was hers."

Phillips said, "Let the record show that the witness has pointed to the defendant, Laurel Adrian."

Phillips held out his hand in a gesture of offering Angela Ryerson to Perry Mason, and sat down.

Mason smiled and took his time approaching the witness stand. He saw that the young girl had shifted her posture to sit up straighter in the chair. He supposed the D.A. had filled her head with dire warnings about the cross-examination and he wanted to relieve any anxieties she might have.

He stopped a few feet in front of her.

"Miss Ryerson," he asked quietly, "when did you first know that your neighbor, Mr. Adrian, had been shot?"

"I—gee, I guess it was a day or two days afterward. I saw the story on television."

"And did you discuss it with anyone at that time, your parents or friends?"

"There was some talk around," she answered. "I don't think I actually discussed it with anyone, though. At first, I think everyone thought it was just a robbery or something."

"Yes. And when did you later remember about seeing Mrs. Adrian's car on that night?"

"It was when the detectives came to my house. They were talking to people in the neighborhood."

"And what did the detectives say? I mean about the shooting."

"Let's see." She had a look of concentration on her face. "They said Mrs. Adrian had been charged with shooting her husband—"

"And that's the first time you knew that fact?"

"Yes, sir."

"You told them then about seeing Mrs. Adrian's car?"

She shook her head. "First, they talked to my parents, then they talked to me. They asked if any of us could remember seeing anything around their house, the house where Mr. and Mrs. Adrian lived, that night."

Mason said, "And you told them about seeing the car?"

She shook her head again. "Not then, because I couldn't be sure which night I saw the car. I mean, I knew it was the night I was baby-sitting at the Hendrens' that I saw the car. When the detectives came around, I didn't know it was so important about the car."

"When did you know it was important?"

"The next day, after the detectives were there. I had talked to my parents. Then my father called them and the detectives came back and I told *them.*"

"Tell me, did you often see Mrs. Adrian in the neighborhood?"

"I wouldn't say, you know, often. But I have seen her some in her car."

Mason nodded encouragingly. "And you knew her car?"

"Oh, yes, sir. It's a neat-looking car. A Lincoln Continental."

Mason smiled. "That's it. Now, do you remember what the weather was like that evening? Can you recall?"

"It was—well, I know I took my umbrella when I went to the Hendrens'," she said slowly, "so it must have been cloudy."

"That's right, it was," Mason agreed. "Overcast. It had been cloudy all day. And according to the weather bureau when I checked with them, it was dark by a few minutes before eight P.M."

"I remember that, too." Angela Ryerson nodded her head vigorously. "The streetlight at the corner was on. That's how I saw her car, under the streetlight."

"And you saw Mrs. Adrian in the car? Driving the car?"

"No, sir. I never said that."

"You never said that?" Mason repeated. "You didn't see who was driving the car, didn't see Mrs. Adrian inside?"

"No, sir," she answered firmly. "The car was beyond the streetlight when it passed me so it was too dark to see who was driving."

Mason was frowning. "Did you tell this to the district attorney, to Mr. Phillips?"

"Yes. Yes, sir, I did. Several times."

Mason thought for a moment. He could, he knew, keep rewording the questions so she would have to keep repeating that she didn't know who was driving the car. Instead, he decided to stop where he was in the cross-examination.

"Thank you, Miss Ryerson. No more questions."

She gave a grateful smile as he turned away.

When Mason reached the defense table, he whispered to Laurel, "I doubt that she did us any damage. If anything, her testimony reinforces the circumstantial aspect of this whole case; to see a car, even if it had been your car, is one thing. Not to see who was driving the car is quite another matter."

She nodded hesitantly. "I had the same feeling, but I couldn't be sure."

"However, here comes some trouble," he said.

He was, he thought, not surprised to see that the next witness to be called by Carter Phillips was Margaret Starke, who lived across the street from the Adrian house in the Hollywood Hills.

Mason had taken note that the D.A. was developing the prosecution's case against Laurel in a more or less straightforward, textbook fashion.

There had been testimony about the scene of the crime, placing Laurel there, about the murder weapon, which she could have used, about her lack of a verifiable alibi for the time of the murder, about the will, which suggested a motive. Now Phillips was going to try to bring forth testimony about quarrels Laurel and her late husband had had.

Carter Phillips asked, "Mrs. Starke, as a close neighbor of Mr. and Mrs. Adrian, what did you observe of their relationship?"

Her head shot up indignantly. "The only thing I ever did notice is that from the time they first moved into the neighborhood, they were always yelling at each other, outside their house, on public display."

"You could hear their voices?"

"Even from inside my house."

"Could you hear their words, hear what they were yelling about?"

"Of course I could," she said, "He would yell at her that she was a flirt."

Mason kept his eyes on Mrs. Starke as she testified. She was a large buxom woman, in her late forties, he guessed, with a face that probably had once been almost pretty but now was plump and permanently petulant.

"He would yell at her that she was a flirt?" Phillips repeated.

"Yes. And she was, too, always parading around outside in skimpy shorts and tight tops, blouses and halters. On public display."

"And you observed that their quarrels continued right up to the time of the murder of Mr. Adrian?"

"Objection!" Mason said. "Mr. Phillips is leading the witness."

"Sustained."

Mrs. Starke looked confused.

Phillips said, "You have stated that the Adrians quarreled from the time they first moved into the neighborhood, is that correct?"

"Yes."

"And for how long a time after they first moved into the neighborhood did they continue to quarrel?"

"Right up until the time of the murder of Mr. Adrian!" she said triumphantly.

"That's all," Phillips said. "Thank you, Mrs. Starke."

Mason didn't particularly relish what he had to do as he advanced toward the witness. Under other circumstances, he might —as the cliché put it—have pitied her more than scorned her. But she had appeared here and made certain possibly damaging statements characterizing Laurel's behavior and he couldn't know for certain what effect, even though small, her words might have. Sometimes, seemingly trivial testimony by a witness could tip the balance between a guilty and not guilty verdict. He knew he had to try to impeach her testimony.

He faced her sternly. "Mrs. Starke, you have just said that the defendant, to use your words, 'always paraded around . . . on public display . . . in skimpy shorts and tight tops, blouses and halters.' Isn't that what you said?"

"I did. Because it's true."

"Would you please tell the court what you mean by 'skimpy shorts'?"

"I mean very tight and very short shorts."

Mason frowned. "I imagine we all have our own opinions about what constitutes 'very tight' and 'very short.' Would you please inform us of your definition of the two terms?"

"I should think it would be obvious to anyone who understands English," she answered sharply.

"The witness will answer counsel's question!" Judge Moorman admonished her, a scowl on his face.

"Yes, sir," Mrs. Starke said, her voice still strident. To Mason, she said, " 'Very tight' means it looked to me like she could barely squeeze into them and 'very short' means it looked to me like the bottoms of the shorts were very high up, up on her—I don't know —thigh, I guess."

"And you would use the same definition for the tops she wore?"

"I only said 'tight' about them," Mrs. Starke said. "And, yes, like she could barely squeeze into them." She sat back in the chair determinedly, as if she had delivered the final word on the subjects.

Mason, however, was not about to let up on her. "Now, when the defendant was dressed in her tights and shorts, she was on the grounds of her own property, is that not so?"

"Yes, outside the house."

" 'On public display,' you said."

"Yes, outside the house is on public display."

"I find that difficult to understand, although you say you observed her?"

"I did. All the time."

"I still find that difficult to understand." Mason's voice was puzzled. "Isn't there a tall hedge—I'd estimate its height at about seven feet—screening the entire grounds in the front of Mrs. Adrian's house?"

"There's a hedge, yes."

"And from the street, it's impossible to see anyone on the grounds, isn't that so?"

"There are other ways to see anyone on the grounds of that house," Mrs. Starke said. "All the houses on the street have at least two stories—"

Mason cut in quickly, "You are saying, then, that you observed

Mrs. Adrian, on her own grounds, dressed casually, *from your upstairs window?*"

"What's wrong with that? So could anyone else who looked, the way she was displaying herself."

"Anyone else who looked, Mrs. Starke? Do you mean your husband?"

"Objection!" Carter Phillips boomed out. "There's been no testimony—"

"I withdraw the question. The witness is excused."

Mason might have been more unhappy with his less-than-gentle cross-examination if, after Carter Phillips told the judge he had no questions on redirect, Mrs. Starke hadn't flounced down from the witness stand and marched away, nose in the air. It would take more than mere gibes to puncture her inborn self-righteousness, Mason thought.

Phillips said, "Your Honor, the State rests."

"Very well," Judge Moorman said. "Since we've gone well into the lunch hour this court is adjourned until tomorrow morning when the defense will begin its rebuttal."

Laurel appeared totally surprised. "That's it?" she asked Mason. "Just like that? They've finished all their charges against me?"

Mason nodded and smiled. "I told you this moment would come."

Della and Drake came to the defense table. Mason stood up. "Let's get out of here."

"Just give me a minute," Laurel said. She had reached into her handbag and taken out a pair of sunglasses.

Mason leaned over her. "Laurel, I think it would be better if you didn't put on the glasses."

She looked up at him. "Whyever in the world not?"

"Well, I'll tell you. They're all going to be waiting outside with their cameras. When the pictures of you show up on TV and in the newspapers, there you'll be with the dark glasses covering your eyes. People who see those pictures will think somehow you have something to hide."

"I never thought of it that way," she said. "But I'll bet you're right."

She put the glasses back into her handbag.

They left the courtroom, Mason and Della on either side of Laurel, Drake a few steps ahead of them to keep curious spectators at a distance. Mason noticed Randolph Adrian and Steven Benedict standing together to one side of the courtroom. Randolph Adrian made a move as if he was going to approach them. Mason quickly took Laurel's arm and led her away from any possibility of being confronted by Randolph Adrian.

The reporters and cameramen were again lined up in front of the building. This time Mason paused only long enough to say "You'll get your real story about this case starting tomorrow."

When some of the reporters kept shouting questions Mason went on to the waiting car without answering.

The driver took Mason, Della, and Drake to their office building and continued on with Laurel to her beach house after Mason gave her a few words of encouragement that he hoped would comfort her.

"For most of the rest of the hearing," he told her, "you will be listening to facts favorable to you, and your defense. After these past few days I'm sure that will be a welcome change for you. I want you to know now that I think you have borne up remarkably well in the courtroom, and that will make a difference in the eyes of the judge. Again, I want to admonish you to get as much rest as you can."

When Mason, Della, and Drake went up to Mason's office, Della asked, "Perry, how do you really think the prosecution's case went over with the judge?"

Mason was emptying the papers from his briefcase onto the desk. Some of the papers fell off onto the floor. Mason bent to retrieve them but Della was already there picking the papers up, saying, "Let me do that, for heaven's sake. You'll get everything out of order. I'll take care of your papers. Take a minute and sit still."

Mason grinned and sat down on his swivel chair. "Thank you, Della. How do I really think the prosecution's case went over? At this point she's still in some jeopardy, I'm afraid."

"It didn't sound to me like the State's presentation was that strong," Drake said.

Mason nodded. "It wasn't. What I think you have to bear in

mind, though, is that up to now the judge has no clear picture of the murder of Gil Adrian except that it appears Laurel shot him."

Della said, "I'll tell you one thing. I don't believe for a second that the judge bought all that stuff Randolph Adrian said, or that Mrs. Starke."

Drake said, "I thought you knocked them right out of the ball park with your cross-exam."

"We scored points," Mason agreed. "But I'm not sure their testimony was all that important to the prosecution to begin with. There is one matter, Paul, you just reminded me of."

"What's that?"

"Obviously, as we learned from the testimony of Mrs. Starke and little Angela Ryerson, the police made a canvass of the Adrian neighborhood to see what kind of information they could uncover. I think we should try the same thing."

"I'll get a team together," Drake said. "We'll go out and beat the bushes this afternoon. Anything else?"

"I can't think of a thing."

"See you, Perry, Della," Drake said on his way out.

Della reached for the papers on Mason's desk. "I'll type up your notes right away."

"Thanks, Della. And Della?"

"Yes, Perry?"

"Would you like to have an early dinner with me tonight?"

"I would like that." She smiled. "I really would."

"Good."

"Just give me time to powder my face."

His phone rang and he waved Della out of the office and picked up the phone.

Gertie said, "Mr. Mason, I have a call for you from a Janet Coleman."

"Yes, all right, put her through."

Janet Coleman came on the line and said, "Mr. Mason, I was in court today to watch you. I just want you to know that I've done some thinking and I think I could testify for you if you need me. I'd like to help Laurel Adrian."

"Fine. I might need your testimony."

"Then consider me available."

Mason thanked her and hung up the phone.

He already had a list of witnesses he had subpoenaed to testify in Laurel's defense. He added Janet Coleman's name to the list and put a question mark after her name.

20

It was raining the next morning when court reconvened at 10
A.M.

"Is the defense ready with its first witness?" Judge Moorman
inquired.

"We are, Your Honor," Perry Mason said. "The defense calls
Mrs. Irene Mitchell."

Mrs. Irene Mitchell lived next door to the Adrian house in the
hills. Drake had talked to her and she was only too happy to testify
for Laurel, so Mason decided to put her on the witness stand first.

"Now, Mrs. Mitchell," Mason said, "how long have you lived in
your present home?"

"Twenty years, Mr. Mason."

She smiled at him and at the court. She was tall, slim, in her
fifties, patrician in appearance, dressed in what looked like a
designer skirt and jacket, a loop of pearls around her throat.

"You were there then when Laurel and Gilbert Adrian moved
into the house next to you?"

"Yes."

"Did you know the Adrians? Were you friends?"

"No. Just good—I would like to think—neighbors."

"You never visited back and forth? Never shared any social life?"

"No," she said. "We introduced ourselves to one another; that is, Mrs. Adrian and I did, soon after they moved in. But beyond that we did not see one another. Socially, that is."

"You did, however, observe the Adrians from time to time, I would imagine."

She nodded. "Yes, of course. Living in somewhat close proximity as we were, it would have been impossible not to. As I'm sure they, or she, at any rate, must have—as you put it—observed us."

"Yes." Mason smiled. "Would you describe, please, what you saw of Laurel Adrian, observed about her general demeanor?"

Irene Mitchell said, "Obviously, most of the times I did see her was when she was outside. She seemed to work quite hard on their flowers, their grounds, the hedge. The place had been vacated for a time before the Adrians moved in and needed a lot of attention and care, which she began giving it almost from the first day they were there."

"Is there anything in particular that you recall about her gardening?"

"Her roses," Irene Mitchell said promptly. "She managed to grow the most beautiful roses. I complimented her on the beauty of her roses one day and soon after she came to my door and presented me with an enormous bouquet of them."

"When you observed her working around the grounds," Mason said, "did you ever feel she was inappropriately dressed?"

"Not at all." The answer was firm. "Sometimes she wore shorts and halters, sometimes slacks."

"She never dressed in a manner you found offensive?"

"Not at all."

"Or provocative, say, to a male eye?"

Irene Mitchell laughed. "I suppose that would depend upon the beholder with the male eye." More seriously, she added, "I can tell you, however, that I don't know how anyone could have seen her at all, behind her hedge, on the grounds, unless they went to a great deal of trouble to look."

"Thank you," Mason said. "Now, did you ever have occasion to overhear Mr. and Mrs. Adrian quarreling? Their voices raised?"

"Once in a while, when he would come home and she was outside, I'd hear him yell at her but I think most married couples do that sometimes. Certainly, my husband and I do."

Mason asked, "And that was about the extent of their exchanges?"

"Yes. And I'll tell you something else; from what I observed of the two of them, she absolutely adored him."

"Objection! The witness is stating an opinion," Carter Phillips said, and it was clear from his tone that he was simply going through a routine motion.

"Sustained."

Mason took a step back. "Thank you, Mrs. Mitchell."

"No questions, Your Honor," Phillips said.

Irene Mitchell stepped down from the witness stand.

Mason swung around to face the judge and said, "The defense calls Melanie Sandford."

Melanie Sandford, who had been sitting in the front row of spectators with Drake, came forward and was sworn in.

Mason led her through a series of statements about her work as a blackjack dealer at The Palms Palace casino-hotel in Las Vegas.

Mason showed her the police photograph of the man who had called himself Karl Braundorff, and asked, "Miss Sandford, have you ever seen this man?"

"Yes, I have—"

"Objection! Objection!" Carter Phillips boomed the words out into the courtroom. "The witness's testimony on this point is irrelevant and immaterial to this hearing."

Mason's tone was mild as he replied, "Several of the People's own witnesses have testified to an involvement of the deceased with this man. And another of the prosecution's chief witnesses, Lieutenant Ray Dallas, has piqued the interest of all of us, I'm sure, by stating that to this day the Los Angeles Police Department does not know the identity of this man. We seek to unravel this mystery inside the larger mystery of who killed Gilbert Adrian."

"Mr. Mason, in what way would this serve the interests of the hearing now before this court?" Judge Moorman asked.

"It seems to me, Your Honor, that since the prosecution has gone to such lengths to establish the timing of the shooting of this man in relation to the timing of the shooting of Gilbert Adrian, it is incumbent upon this court—"

"Objection!" Phillips said sharply. "The timing of the two incidents *is* material and relevant—"

"Your Honor," Mason cut in, "may I please finish my statement?"

"Mr. Phillips, Mr. Mason," Judge Moorman said sternly, "you each will kindly do the other the courtesy of letting him complete a sentence before you interrupt. Mr. Phillips, I have your objection under consideration. I would now like to have Mr. Mason complete his statement. Then I'll rule. Continue, Mr. Mason."

"It seems to me that it is as incumbent upon this court to attempt to bring to the light of truth all we can discover about this man as it was incumbent to establish that he was a corpse only after testimony that certain bullets had been removed from his body."

Mason paused to try to gauge the effect of his argument on the judge and decided to add, "In addition, for the record, I would like to point out that it was the prosecution and its witnesses who introduced the subject into this case, allowing for proper further inquiry by the defense. Or so it seems to me."

Judge Moorman considered his words for a moment before he said, "Mr. Phillips, your objection is not without possible merit. But I think the key element to Mr. Mason's argument is that the People *did* introduce the subject and it *is* a part of the case. The witness may answer."

Mason was quietly elated. He had managed to open the door to testimony not only by Melanie Sandford but also by Janet Coleman and Anselmo Costa, and thus had laid the groundwork for offering the possibility that one or more persons other than Laurel might have had reason to shoot and kill Gilbert Adrian.

He returned to his examination of Melanie Sandford.

"To repeat the question, Miss Sandford: Have you ever seen the man in the photograph?"

"I have, yes."

"And where and when have you seen him?"

"I have seen him frequently in the casino of The Palms Palace in Las Vegas where I worked. He was there for about two weeks, in the casino every night."

"When was this, exactly?"

"The last few days of April and the first week of May of this year."

"As you know, as we have heard from the testimony of the prosecution's witness, he was shot and killed on the night of May eleventh of this year, which would have been just shortly after you saw him in Las Vegas."

"Yes." Melanie Sandford nodded.

"At the time you saw him, did you observe him in the company of any particular individual?"

"I did, yes. Most of the time he was with Mr. Anselmo Costa in the casino."

"Anselmo Costa," Mason repeated. "Anselmo Costa."

He nodded at Melanie Sandford. "No more questions."

"Mr. Phillips?" Judge Moorman asked.

"No questions."

The judge inclined his head toward Mason. "Call your next witness."

Mason had anticipated there would be a reaction in the courtroom when his next witness appeared so he was not surprised at the murmurs when he said, "The defense calls Janet Coleman."

Mason glanced at the defense table. He had informed Laurel in advance that he intended to call Janet Coleman and had instructed Laurel to try to retain her composure. He saw she was sitting quietly.

He turned to Janet Coleman as she sat down after being sworn in.

"Miss Coleman, did you know the deceased, Gilbert Adrian?"

Carter Phillips stood up and Mason expected an objection, but instead, Phillips sat down as abruptly as he had risen.

"I knew Mr. Adrian, yes. We were acquaintances."

Mason nodded. When he had spoken with Janet Coleman earlier that morning they had determined she could testify without revealing she was working undercover for the federal government.

"Were you ever in Las Vegas with Gilbert Adrian?"

"I was. Several times. At The Palms Palace casino-hotel."

"When was the last time you were there with Gilbert Adrian?"

"April twenty-first, twenty-second, and twenty-third. We arrived there the twenty-first, stayed through the following day and night, and returned on the twenty-third."

"Was there a particular person Gilbert Adrian spent time with at The Palms Palace casino-hotel?"

"Oh, yes." She nodded. "Every time we were there Gilbert Adrian spent some time with Anselmo Costa. On occasion I saw them exchange large sums of money, so I assumed they had a business relationship—"

"Objection!" Carter Phillips said. "Conjecture on the part of the witness."

"Sustained."

The judge looked at Janet Coleman. "The witness will confine her answers to what she knows, not what she assumes."

Mason was satisfied. He said, "No further questions."

Carter Phillips shook his head. "No questions."

Mason watched Janet Coleman walk away and called his next witness. "Anselmo Costa."

Costa, who had been sitting in the rear of the courtroom with his lawyer, Graham Kendrick, came forward and was sworn in by the clerk.

"Mr. Costa, there has been testimony in this court that you were acquainted with this man"—Mason held out the police photograph—"who called himself Karl Braundorff. Did you know him?"

Costa ignored the photograph and Mason laid it on the top of the witness stand.

Costa said, "I respectfully decline to answer any questions on the grounds that my answers might tend to incriminate me."

"Mr. Costa, did you know the man in this photograph, who called himself Karl Braundorff?"

"I respectfully decline to answer any questions on the grounds that my answers might tend to incriminate me."

Judge Moorman pounded his gavel and rose up from the bench to say to Anselmo Costa, "You, sir, will answer counsel's questions or this court will hold you in contempt!"

Mason said again, "Mr. Costa, did you know the man in this photograph, who called himself Karl Braundorff?"

Costa glared at Mason. "I refuse to answer any questions on the grounds that my answers might tend to incriminate me—"

"Marshall!" Judge Moorman called out. "You will take this witness into custody and escort him to the city jail." The judge looked at Anselmo Costa. "You, sir, will be held in contempt of court for as long as this hearing lasts. Or until you testify in these proceedings."

One of the city marshals stationed at the rear of the courtroom came forward, handcuffed Costa, and led him away.

Judge Moorman pounded his gavel again. "This court will take a thirty-minute recess."

Mason walked back to the defense table. Della and Drake came forward from the row of seats where they had been observing the proceedings and talked with Mason at the defense table.

"Thanks, Perry, for giving Costa a taste of his own medicine," Drake said, grinning. "I like the idea of him being locked up behind bars, even if it's just for a short time. Now he'll know how I felt in Las Vegas."

Mason grinned, too. "I think you should feel a kind of poetic justice in that turn of events, Paul."

Drake said, "Not bad, either, the way you managed to let the judge know that Gil Adrian could have had other people who might want him dead."

"I can't say I'm not pleased," Mason agreed. "Melanie Sandford and Janet Coleman made credible witnesses, too. And so did Irene Mitchell. She was very helpful to us, Paul, and we wouldn't have had her if you hadn't found her."

"I'll tell you one thing, Perry," Della said. "Mrs. Mitchell's testimony sure wiped out any damage done to Laurel by that Starke woman."

"I would like to think so."

Drake said, "Perry, don't you feel encouraged by the ways things have gone for you this morning? I think you should."

Mason was glancing around the courtroom where many of the spectators had remained in their seats during the recess. He saw that Melanie Sandford and Janet Coleman were talking together. He spotted Megan Calder sitting alone.

She would be his next witness. He noticed Randolph Adrian and Steven Benedict huddled together near the rear doors. And, he was surprised to note, John Fallon, manager of the Oaks Restaurant, had returned to the courtroom to follow the hearing.

Mason looked back at Drake and, in answer to Drake's last question, said, "Do I feel encouraged by the way things have gone this morning?"

He paused and shrugged.

"The way I view this criminal hearing, any criminal hearing," he said, "is in terms of the myth of Sisyphus. Do you remember your Greek mythology? Sisyphus was a legendary king of Corinth who was condemned forever to roll a heavy stone up a steep hill in Hades only to have the stone roll down again as it neared the top."

He smiled wryly at Della and Drake before he continued. "In a criminal hearing I view evidence as that heavy stone. And for a while it is the prosecutor who must take the place of Sisyphus and roll it up a steep hill. Then, partway up, it becomes the turn of the defense to take over the task—but with an important difference. Now the stand-in for Sisyphus not only must keep the huge stone from rolling down and crushing him but also must chip away at it piece by piece until it's demolished."

He looked at Della and Drake who were staring at him with rapt expressions. He tried to lighten the portentousness of his words by smiling as he added, "Don't let the prosecutor ever hear that I suggested he was a stand-in for Sisyphus. He'd probably accuse me of calling him a dirty name."

Mason waved them away good-naturedly and sat alone to review his notes for the examination of Megan Calder until Judge Moorman returned and Megan Calder took the stand.

"How long were you employed as Gilbert Adrian's secretary?" Mason asked.

"For seven years and two months. From the time Adrian Enterprises first went into business up until a few days ago. When I was told my services were no longer required."

Mason deliberately delayed his next question, hoping she would add one more line to her answer. And then she said, "Mr. Randolph Adrian so informed me."

Good girl! Mason thought, knowing Carter Phillips would have asked her a question that would have elicited the same answer at the conclusion of the cross-examination. And thus would have undercut some of the testimony she had given by making it ap-

pear she had appeared as a defense witness because she felt
spiteful toward the company.

"As you were Gilbert Adrian's secretary, he of course confided
certain matters to you during that time?"

"Yes."

"Now, would you tell the court, exactly as you told me, why you
first came to my office to talk to me."

She looked at the judge and the jury as she spoke. "I wanted to
help Mrs. Adrian if I could."

"Were you friends with Laurel Adrian?"

"Never. I only saw her and spoke to her when she came into the
office."

"But you wanted to help her."

"Yes. Because I thought I knew some things that perhaps no
one else ever knew."

"Go on."

"For instance, Mr. Adrian told me something once about the
safe he had at his house. There was money he kept there, cash,
lots of it."

"He told you this?"

"He told me, yes. And since I never learned from the news that
there was any money taken from the house, I assume nobody else
knew about it."

Mason was aware of a sudden stir in the courtroom.

"Thank you." Mason handed her the appointment book she
had left with him. "Do you recognize this?"

"It was an appointment book kept by Mr. Adrian."

"His only appointment book?"

"No, sir." Megan Calder shook her head. "He had a regular
appointment book at the office in which he and I both made
entries."

"And were you aware of the existence of this second appointment book?"

"Not until I cleaned out his desk, after he died."

"And have you compared the entries in the two books?"

"I have," she said.

"Are the entries similar?"

"Not exactly, sir."

"How do they differ?"

"In this book, the one he kept in his desk drawer, there are two sets of entries. One is for appointments for each day that exactly match the entries in the book he kept on his desk, the book I knew about."

"And the other set of entries?" Mason asked.

"They're enclosed in parentheses, where they appear. And the entries in parentheses, which are for totally different appointments, are for the same times and dates as the entries opposite them."

"And you have no explanation for this?"

"No. None."

Mason smiled. "Would you please turn to the appointment entries in this book for the date of May eleventh. Do you have it?"

"Yes, May eleventh—"

"Now, would you look down the page to the entry for five-fifteen P.M."

"Yes, I have it. There's only one entry, which has a line drawn through it. That entry reads 'Catlin' and—"

"Excuse me," Mason interrupted. "Catlin, that was Mr. Adrian's lawyer?"

"Yes. William Catlin."

"Please proceed."

Megan Calder glanced down at the book again. "And the new entry reads 'Dayton.' That would be Jerome Dayton, Mr. Adrian's accountant."

"From these two entries it would appear that Gilbert Adrian had intended to see his lawyer, William Catlin, on the afternoon of the eleventh and then changed the appointment to meet with Jerome Dayton instead. Since we have had testimony from the prosecution's witness, Lieutenant Dallas, that it has been verified Gilbert Adrian *did* visit Jerome Dayton on that date at that time, it would seem the appointment had been changed."

"It would seem so, yes," Megan Calder answered.

Mason said, "Now, we have had testimony from Randolph Adrian that his father phoned his lawyer on May eleventh and made an appointment to see the lawyer on May twelfth about his will—"

Megan Calder was looking at the book. "May twelfth, five-fifteen P.M. 'Catlin' it says."

Mason said, "The appointment he had changed from May eleventh when he planned to change his will—"

"Objection!" Phillips said angrily. "Your Honor, we do not have testimony that Gilbert Adrian planned to change his will on the previous date."

"Your Honor," Mason said quickly, "we will have such testimony shortly, I assure you."

"I will withhold a ruling on that basis," Judge Moorman said. "But I warn you, Mr. Mason, you had better produce that testimony."

"I shall, Your Honor," Mason said. He added, "I have completed my examination of this witness."

Carter Phillips asked his first question of Megan Calder as he walked toward the front of the courtroom. "You have testified that Gilbert Adrian told you he kept large sums of cash in his safe at home, is that correct?"

"Yes."

"Was anyone else aware of this fact, to your knowledge?"

"To my knowledge, no."

"After his death, didn't it occur to you to go to the police with this information?"

Megan Calder said, "As far as I knew, the police could already have uncovered that information."

"But you went to see Mr. Mason?"

"I did. Because, as I testified just moments ago, I wanted to help Laurel Adrian."

"And you thought if it was known that the money was missing, it would hurt Laurel Adrian?"

"I didn't know. So I went to see Mr. Mason." She raised her voice. "And he told me to tell the police, whether it would help Laurel Adrian or hurt her."

The D.A. paused, then said, "We have heard testimony from you about this alleged secret appointment book Adrian kept with its double entries enclosed in parentheses, as I believe you told this court."

He looked at her intently. She answered, "Yes."

Phillips said, "I confess I couldn't deduce the significance of your testimony on the matter of the double entries. Have they some particular significance that has escaped me?"

Megan Calder looked straight back at him. "I don't know. I sure would like to find out. I was simply testifying to what was a fact, hoping, I suppose, that somebody would provide an explanation that would make sense."

It was obvious that Carter Phillips was undecided whether to pursue the possible meaning of the double entries with her or drop the whole subject.

Finally, he said, "The witness is excused."

Mason was on his feet immediately, calling for his next witness. He had seen the judge watching the clock and he wanted to question William Catlin, who had been Gilbert Adrian's lawyer, before court was recessed.

Catlin, who was in his forties, of medium height, with dark, wavy hair, sat in the witness chair at ease when Mason nodded to him prior to the opening question.

"Do you recall the appointment your client, Gilbert Adrian, made with you for five-fifteen P.M., May eleventh?"

"I do. I have read over my log to refresh my memory."

"Would you tell the court what the purpose of that meeting was to be?"

"When Mr. Adrian made the appointment he told me he wanted to make arrangements to change his will."

Mason nodded. "And did you and Mr. Adrian, in fact, meet on the date of May eleventh?"

Catlin shook his head. "On the afternoon of May eleventh, Mr. Adrian phoned me and changed the appointment to the following day; that is, to May twelfth."

Mason looked up at Judge Moorman. "The defense has no further questions, Your Honor."

"No questions," Carter Phillips said.

"Mr. Mason, do you have other witnesses?" Judge Moorman asked. "If so, we'll adjourn for the weekend."

Mason still hadn't decided whether or not to put Laurel on the stand. But he didn't want to lose the opportunity without careful consideration. He said, "Your Honor, the defense requests a continuance."

"Very well. This hearing is adjourned until Monday morning."

21

Perry Mason walked into his apartment at a few minutes before 11 P.M. after having dinner with Della Street.

Rain was still pouring down outside as it had been all day.

His clothes were damp and he was weary. He put his briefcase down and went to the kitchen to fix a cup of coffee. On the way he flipped on the television set.

When he came back into the living room with his coffee and sank gratefully into a plush chair, he saw that the late news was coming on. The sound was turned down and he glanced at the screen without much interest. There were pictures of the president greeting some foreign dignitary in front of the White House, pictures of a bombing in Northern Ireland, pictures of a plane crash in Africa, and then there were pictures of the Los Angeles Courthouse, of Carter Phillips, of Laurel Adrian, of Mason himself as they had left court earlier that day.

The pictures on the TV screen changed to a series of sketch drawings of the various participants in the trial, drawn by Della Street's least favorite sketch artist. He gathered they were doing a summary story on the trial.

He moved to turn up the sound and the phone rang. He picked up the phone.

"Mason."

"Mr. Mason, this is Laurel Adrian," came the words through the receiver in a breathless rush. "Thank God you're finally there! There's been some terrible trouble. Can you come at once? Please?"

Mason was still watching the television screen as one sketch drawing after another appeared: Judge Moorman, Laurel, Carter Phillips—Della was right: They all looked as if they had beards—Randolph Adrian, Mason, Margaret Starke, Gilbert Adrian, Anselmo Costa . . .

"Come where?" Mason, distracted momentarily by the pictures on the TV screen, asked.

"I'm at—at Randolph Adrian's house—"

"Randolph Adrian's house?" Mason was incredulous. "What are you doing there?"

"I can't tell you now. When you get here. Please hurry! Please! I'm in trouble."

"Why? What's happened?"

"Something terrible. I don't think we should discuss it now on the phone. You just have to come." There was no doubting the anxiety and fear in her voice.

"All right, I'll be there right away. Give me the address."

He jotted down the street name and number and looked back at the TV screen. Despite Laurel's alarming call, he was disturbed by an entirely different perplexity. There had been something—and he didn't know what it was—he had seen on television that had triggered an urgent reaction in him. He had spotted something and Laurel's words had knocked it right out of his mind. But whatever it had been remained tantalizingly just beyond the reach of his memory, of his thoughts. He could only hope he could recall it, given time, because he was convinced it had been important. He pulled on his raincoat, which still had beads of water on it, jammed the note with the address on it into a coat pocket, and went out of the apartment.

The rain was coming down in sheets, foreshortening the view through the windshield, and he drove at a moderate speed when he turned onto the Hollywood Freeway.

He could not imagine what had put Laurel in such a state unless she had remembered some information that might come out in her cross-examination on Monday and convict her of her husband's death.

Driving through the heavy rain he was glad he had had a chance to drink a cup of coffee while he had been home. The coffee helped dull his fatigue.

The address Laurel had given him for Randolph Adrian's house was in West Hollywood, off Sunset Boulevard.

Once off the freeway Mason increased his speed. When he pulled up in front of the house he saw there were lights on inside the place, a modest-looking single-story ranch-type house with a white picket fence in front.

While he was still getting out of the car Laurel came running out of the front door, unmindful of the rain although she wore no coat, and her dress and hair were almost instantly soaked and dripping.

She ran to him and clutched his arm. "Oh, Mr. Mason, it's so awful!"

"What's the trouble?" Mason asked.

Her hand was trembling as she led him up the walkway.

"Ju-ju-ju-just look for yourself," she stammered.

He walked swiftly ahead of her through the open front door.

Randolph Adrian lay slumped over a refectory table in the living room. A small crystal chandelier hung directly over the table. The light shining down reflected off the silver handle of the letter opener plunged into Adrian's back. Mason felt for a pulse in Adrian's throat. There was none. Mason straightened and strode back to Laurel, who was standing just inside the open front door. He slammed the door shut.

Laurel was trembling so violently he was afraid she might faint.

He took her by the shoulders and said, "Calm down. You have to talk to me. I have to know what's happened."

She nodded her head several times before she finally was able to get the words out, "I—he phoned me earlier this evening. Randolph did. He said it was important that he see me. Important to me, he said. He said he had some—some evidence that would —would clear me. But that we had to get some matters cleared up about—about his father's will. He insisted it had to be done right away, tonight."

"You should never have agreed to see him alone," Mason said.

"I know." She nodded. "But he kept saying it had to be tonight and that he wouldn't call me again. That I either had to agree or it was no deal. 'No deal' were the words he used. I agreed to see him. I thought I could phone you in the meantime and you'd be here, too. But I tried to call you again and again and there was no answer."

"All right," Mason said impatiently. "You couldn't reach me. So what happened? What time did you get here?"

"About a half hour ago. He was there. Dead."

"How did you get in?"

"All the lights were on. I rang the bell. When there was no answer, I tried the door. It was unlocked. I came in and found him."

"Have you called the police yet?"

"Yes, just a few minutes ago. When I thought you'd have time to get here."

She looked miserable. "I didn't know what to do. I kept trying to call you before I called them."

"All right, you've said that before."

She paused for a moment. "I think I saw a car driving away just as I got here."

Mason glanced at her sharply. She stared back unblinking.

"Did you touch anything in the house?"

"No," she said. "Except the phone, trying to call you."

"This is important," Mason said. "Are you sure about the time?"

"I guess just before eleven o'clock. Because when I finally did reach you, I glanced at the clock to get an idea of what time you might get here. That was only a few minutes after eleven."

Mason shook his head. "The police will want to know why you waited. And they won't like it that you waited until you thought I'd get here. But we'll deal with that."

He glanced around the room and then back at her.

"Listen to me carefully," he told her. "You can't guess about the time. When the police question you, you must know for sure what time it was. Do you understand?"

"Yes," she said. "It was just before eleven o'clock." She bit her lip nervously. "What do I say when they ask me why I called you before I called them?"

Mason thought for a moment. "That shouldn't be a problem—under the circumstances you were already in. Having gone through a grilling and indictment for your husband's murder, naturally you would want to call me before you called the police."

Mason glanced out the window when he saw red lights flashing outside. He said, "Speaking of which, I think they're here."

She started trembling again.

Mason asked matter-of-factly, "At the time you got here, you said you thought you saw a car driving away."

"I think I did," she said slowly. "I couldn't see what kind of car it was or who was in it."

She jumped when there was a loud pounding on the door.

"Listen," Mason said roughly. "You saw another car drive away, or you didn't, do you understand? No guessing about it."

She looked at him intently. "I did. I saw another car drive away as I was arriving."

"All right," Mason said. "Go let them in."

As he watched her walk toward the door, Mason knew that once the police entered this house they would pull out all stops to try to indict Laurel Adrian for another murder.

He knew the best thing for him to do was stand quietly, as a heavyset plainclothesman came through the door and confronted Laurel. Laurel had put on her sunglasses. The plainclothesman held up a wallet with a shield attached. "Sergeant Mel Anders, Homicide. We got a report of a murder at this address."

"Yes." Laurel nodded, visibly shaken. "I made the phone call."

Anders moved on into the room and was followed by a second plainclothesman and two uniformed patrolmen. All four police officers were wary as they eyed Laurel and then Mason.

Mason stepped forward. "I'm Perry Mason, an attorney, and this is Mrs. Laurel Adrian." He turned toward the refectory table. "The victim's there."

Anders and his partner circled around Mason and approached the body slumped over the table. The two patrolmen stood, backs to the door, their eyes on Laurel and Mason.

"His name was Randolph Adrian," Mason said as the two detectives stood looking at Adrian's body. "This is his house."

Anders said something to his partner, who went to the phone and called the station house.

Anders himself stayed for a long time silently looking at the dead man from various angles before he came back to Mason and Laurel.

"All right," he said, "suppose you tell me what happened here."

Mason said, "Mrs. Adrian discovered the body. She's Randolph Adrian's stepmother. She received a phone call earlier this evening from Randolph Adrian asking her to come to the house."

Anders held up a hand. "Suppose we let the lady tell it herself."

Laurel looked at Mason. He nodded.

She told her story to Anders. The sergeant made notes as she talked. Mason listened, face impassive, as she spoke. Now and then Anders glanced at Mason as if he expected an interruption. Since Laurel related the same account to Anders as she had to Mason, Mason felt there was no need to inject himself into the exchange between them.

It was clear, from the expression on the homicide sergeant's face, that he was skeptical of the story Laurel told him. He swung around suddenly to face Mason.

"How did you get here before the police arrived?"

"You heard what Mrs. Adrian told you. She phoned me as soon as she walked in and discovered the body and then she phoned the police."

"I guess what I want to know," Anders said with mock exasperation, "is why she would phone you *before* she phoned the police—"

The sergeant had no time to finish the question. His partner had completed the phone call to the station house and had grabbed Anders by the sleeve and pulled him away. Mason winked at Laurel, trying to reassure her. The two detectives whispered together for several minutes.

Anders walked back. He said, "I just got orders from the precinct. My instructions are to request that you remain here, Mrs. Adrian, Mr. Mason."

Mason shrugged. He suspected that the sergeant had just been informed exactly who Laurel and he were, and who Randolph Adrian had been.

"Just take it easy," Mason said to Laurel when Sergeant Anders wandered away to take another look at the body and the refectory table, along with his partner.

Mason deliberately headed in the opposite direction, toward a front window. He peered out as if he were impatient. The two patrolmen still stood watch inside the front door.

Mason went through an elaborate pantomime at the window, of looking out, glancing at his watch, and then at Anders and the other detective. Finally he went over to Anders and said, indignation in his voice, "What is this, Sergeant? Mrs. Adrian and I are not going to stay around here all night! If you have any further questions, ask them. She and I both have done everything the law requires under the circumstances."

The sergeant seemed taken aback. He said, "Hey, hold on, now! You haven't done *everything*. I requested that you remain here. Those were my instructions."

"And if we choose not to?"

"Then, I'll take you both into the station house for a formal statement," Anders said brusquely.

Mason wasn't really listening. He had put on his show of annoyance simply to enable him to get close enough to observe Randolph Adrian's body and the area around it. He wanted to see if he could spot any clue or clues before the forensic team, the medical examiner, and the other detectives arrived.

On the surface of the refectory table were a pen and a bank checkbook and a couple of letter envelopes, sealed, lying facedown. There were also several other envelopes, slit open, lying on the desk. He wandered away from the table and saw a wicker wastepaper basket with a newspaper stuffed into it. He paused long enough to note that the date on the newspaper was several weeks old.

"Mason!" Anders called out sharply. "Don't touch anything!"

"I know better than that, Sergeant," he answered. He walked back to where Laurel was sitting.

There was a long wait before from outside came the sound of cars driving up and the house quickly filled with men moving back and forth in the living room. Mason and Laurel were ignored until finally, as Mason had expected, Lieutenant Ray Dallas came striding through the door.

Dallas acknowledged Mason's presence with the barest nod of

the head, went directly to Randolph Adrian's body, and stood conferring with Sergeant Anders. Now and then the two men cast a look at Mason and Laurel. Their talk finished, Dallas whirled and bore down on them.

"All right," Dallas said, wasting no words. "I've heard from Sergeant Anders what you have to say, Mrs. Adrian. And you, too, Mason. I'm telling you straight out there's something fishy about this whole business."

Mason said mildly, "I couldn't agree more, Lieutenant."

"I mean about you being here with your client before the police got here."

Mason gave a wave of dismissal with his hand. "I think it was perfectly logical for Mrs. Adrian to call me, especially considering what she's going through in court. Naturally, she was shaken when she arrived here and found yet another murder."

He put a hand on Laurel's arm. "Lieutenant, as you can see, Mrs. Adrian is exhausted. She's told you all she knows. How about letting her go home now and get some rest? You know she's not going to disappear on you. When you've finished collecting all your evidence here, she'll be glad to answer any further questions."

Dallas considered for a moment. "All right, okay, she can leave for now. But I want you to stick around for a while."

"Fair enough."

Mason walked Laurel to the door and stood there until she drove away.

In the living room, Lieutenant Dallas was taking a careful look at the body.

Mason joined him and said, "What do you think, Ray?"

Dallas was studying the silver letter opener protruding from Randolph Adrian's back. "It would appear he was here at the desk, opening his mail, writing checks, and someone, perhaps your client, got behind him and stabbed him."

Mason, curious, asked, "I wonder where those two envelopes were headed?" He pointed to the sealed envelopes lying facedown.

Dallas took a pencil from his pocket and flipped the two envelopes faceup. One was addressed to the telephone company, the other to an insurance company.

"Bills," Dallas said. He used the pencil to flip through the check stubs in the bank book. One, for check number 322, recorded payment to the telephone company. The next stub, for check number 323, noted payment to the California Statewide Insurance Company. There was no notation on the next check stub. The next unused check, with the bank name and Randolph Adrian's name and address printed on it, was number 325.

Mason moved away from the table and, as if noticing for the first time the newspaper stuffed into the wicker wastepaper basket, said, "That's curious."

"What? What's curious?" Dallas asked, hurrying over.

Mason pointed. "According to the date on it, that newspaper is several weeks old."

The lieutenant pulled out the newspaper. The date on it was April 23. The paper was turned to an inside page. On the page was a photograph of a familiar figure with the caption PROMINENT BUSINESSMAN GILBERT ADRIAN AT GROUNDBREAKING CEREMONY YESTERDAY FOR NEW MUNICIPAL GARAGE.

Dallas looked up from the newspaper and shrugged. "It's just an old newspaper with a photograph of Gilbert Adrian. So what?"

"But why would Randolph Adrian have it here, stuffed in a wastepaper basket? There are no other newspapers around."

"Beats me." Suddenly Dallas glanced at Mason suspiciously. "Say, what are you trying to pull, Mason? You planted this here for me to find, didn't you?"

"I don't know what you're talking about, Lieutenant. Why would I want to plant an old newspaper somewhere where you'd find it?"

"To create a 'red herring,' for one thing," Dallas said hotly. "To throw me off the track, maybe. It would be a cute trick."

"I didn't plant the newspaper. I haven't tried to pull any cute tricks."

"Then maybe your client did," Dallas said grimly. "Lord knows she was here long enough before the police got here to have manufactured any number of pieces of evidence."

"She wouldn't have done it, Ray. I'm certain."

"The whole business is still fishy. And the only thing I'm certain about is that from everything I see this murder's almost exactly a replay of her husband's murder, as far as her story is concerned."

Mason said, "She could be innocent, Ray. Somebody could have set her up."

Dallas shook his head stubbornly. "I don't see much here that says she could be innocent. The same evidence that applied in her husband's case applies in this one."

Dallas took a deep breath and enumerated. "She had the opportunity. She—despite what she says—could have gotten Randolph Adrian to agree to meet her here on some pretext or another. She could have told him she wanted to talk to him about cutting him in on the will. She had the means, stabbing him in the back with the letter opener. And she had the motive. She wanted him out of the way so he couldn't make any trouble about the will."

"All circumstantial, Ray," Mason pointed out.

"She planned it that way. *And* she figured nobody would think she would dare commit another murder while she was already in the middle of a pretrial hearing for the first murder. She counted on confusing everyone."

Mason rubbed his eyes. "Ray, what I think is confusing everyone is that there have been too many murders surrounding the corpus delicti—the body of the crime—of the murder of Gilbert Adrian."

Mason took a step away. "At any rate, if you don't need me any longer, I'm going."

"Go," Dallas said. "I wish I could."

The rain was still falling as Mason drove slowly away from Randolph Adrian's house and headed home. The car's headlights bored a path through the glistening sheet of rain gusting across the road.

He drove more cautiously than usual because a part of his mind was trying to puzzle out the events of the night.

Laurel's story had been none too credible—even to him. Was it that she was a quick thinker who always had an answer for everything, or was it that at every turn she was an unusually unfortunate victim of incriminating circumstances in both murders? Whichever it was, she had certainly made sure that he had his work cut out for him in trying to defend her.

He shook his head in annoyance when he remembered how she had put on those damn dark sunglasses of hers as soon as the police appeared. They made her look guilty of something even if she was innocent. The police, especially good detectives like Ray Dallas, weren't stupid about such matters as the attempts people made to conceal themselves with obvious disguises. The clothes people chose to wear were one such form of concealment, along with hats, with—as was once the case with women—veils, with beards, with hairstyles, and with sunglasses.

Mason wondered about the checkbook lying on the rectory table next to Randolph Adrian's body, and about the out-of-date newspaper stuffed into the wastepaper basket. Had Laurel planted them so they would be found and serve—as Dallas put it about the newspaper—as a 'red herring'?

Mason remembered then with a sudden shock of recognition what it was that had eluded him when Laurel's phone call had interrupted him earlier while he was watching the sketch drawings during the summary report of the trial on television.

He grabbed up the car telephone.

Paul Drake, Jr.'s voice was sleepy when he answered the call, "For Pete's sake, Perry, do you know what time it is?"

"How did you know it was me calling?"

"Nobody else ever calls me at this hour of the night. Most other people except you have the good sense to be in bed."

"You can go back to sleep in a minute," Mason said. "I've got a job that needs to be done first thing in the morning. I need a photographic exhibit made in a hurry and I'm not even sure it can be done. Be at my office at eight A.M. I'll give you all the details then."

"Tomorrow's Sunday," Drake said.

"That's why I want you at the office at eight A.M. If the exhibit works out the way I hope, I'll need it in court first thing Monday morning."

22

Della Street said, "Here are all the notes you wanted typed up for use in court tomorrow."

She laid the pages on Mason's desk.

"Good girl." Mason put the stack of papers into his briefcase.

His eyes were bloodshot and his face gray with fatigue. Yet there was still about him an air of determined concentration. A sure sign to anyone who knew him as well as Della did that his mind was preoccupied with a dozen different angles of a complicated problem.

Mason closed his briefcase and glanced at his watch. "Good Lord, Della," he said apologetically, "it's almost eight P.M. It's bad enough to have to ask you to work on a Sunday without keeping you here to all hours. Let's call it a day."

"I won't argue with you on that one," Della said, "if you're sure you have everything you need for tomorrow."

"Thanks to you I do."

Mason stood and stretched and his telephone rang.

Della leaned across the desk and answered, "Perry Mason's office."

She handed the receiver to Mason. "It's Paul."

Mason sat on a corner of his desk as he took the telephone. "Yes, Paul?"

Drake's voice sounded far away. "Listen, Perry, there's been a new development in the case. This one's a honey! I'm in a bar a couple of miles from Laurel Adrian's beach house. I don't want to say any more over the phone. I think you'd better get over here in a hurry!"

Mason jotted down the address Drake gave him. He said, "I'll be right there. Hang on a minute, Paul. What's the latest on that exhibit I need for tomorrow?"

Drake rushed his words. "I left the photographic studio about an hour ago. The guy I got to agree to do the job's still working on it. He promised he'll have it done—if it can be done—by the morning."

"Okay, Paul. I'm on my way."

Mason hung up the phone.

Della was looking at him questioningly. "Something's come up," he said. "I have to meet Paul in a bar. Let's go!"

Della followed him out of the office, turning off the lights and locking the door behind them.

Downstairs, Mason flagged down a taxicab and sent Della home, saying he'd see her at the courthouse in the morning.

At a few minutes before 9 P.M. he walked into the dimly lighted bar off the Pacific Coast Highway and found Drake waiting for him. Drake grabbed him by the arm and pulled him into a corner just inside the door.

"See that guy over there?" Drake pointed. "Recognize him?"

Mason studied the man hunched over a table near the bar, a half-filled glass and bottle of whiskey in front of him.

"Should I?" Mason asked.

"That's Charley Dumas. The private investigator we've been tailing while he's been tailing Laurel Adrian."

"Okay. Go on."

"About two hours ago I got a phone call from my operative, Sam Baylor, who's been keeping tabs on Dumas. Sam was here at the bar. He said he thought I'd better get right over here. I did and Sam told me he'd followed Dumas out to Laurel Adrian's house earlier. Her car was in the drive and the lights were on in the house. Sam kept watch on Dumas, from a distance, while Dumas kept watch on the house. After a time a funny thing happened. Sam saw another car drive up and park behind the car Dumas was in. A man got out, went to Dumas, talked to him for several minutes, and Dumas took off in a hurry. Sam waited only long enough to see that the man who had spoken to Dumas went into the house. Then Sam followed Dumas here to the bar."

"All right." Mason nodded. "Let's hear the rest of it."

"Sam recognized the man who talked to Dumas and then went into the house," Drake said. "Lieutenant Frank Latham."

"Latham? Latham went into Laurel's house?"

Drake said, "Like they say, you ain't heard nothing yet."

Drake grinned. "As soon as Sam told me the story, I sent him back out to the house and went to work on Dumas here, standing him to drinks. Dumas sure likes to drink. Plus it was easy to see he was all shook up. We got to be real buddies, Charley and I, talking about the old days, about both of us being private investigators. He never connected it up that I was working for you and Laurel Adrian and pretty soon he's had enough to drink that he suggests he and I team up on this deal he's got going. He says he'll cut me in for a piece if I agree to help him. Guess what the deal is?"

"Something unsavory, I'd wager."

Drake nodded and grinned again. "The way he put it was that he had information to sell that would be valuable to a certain party if they knew nobody would ever hear about it."

"Blackmail, in other words?"

"That's the name I'd call it."

"And the certain party he wanted to sell it to would be Laurel Adrian," Mason said.

"Right on the mark," Drake answered. "Only I didn't get that out of him until after some more drinks and after I told him I'd like to be cut in on the deal. And after I asked him what I was supposed to do for my share. He told me that tonight his cover had been blown in keeping an eye on the potential customer for his information. He said this cop—meaning Lieutenant Latham—had happened along and had spotted him watching Laurel Adrian's house. The cop, not knowing who he was or who he was working for, scared Charley off, warning him that he was interfering in a police matter, and to stay away from Laurel Adrian and the house. That's why Charley wanted me to help him and to take his place tailing her."

Mason narrowed his eyes. "And exactly what was this valuable information he had that he wanted to sell to Laurel?"

"It took a lot more drinks before I got that out of him," Drake said wearily. "He says she's got a boyfriend, that she had a boyfriend even before her husband was murdered. He's been following her around, trying to find out who the boyfriend is before he approaches her. He thinks she ought to pay plenty if he sells the information to her instead of giving it to anyone else, especially since she's on trial for her husband's murder."

"How does he say he knew about her boyfriend?"

Drake said, "Simple. He says about a month before the murder Gilbert Adrian hired him. Adrian told him he suspected his wife was cheating on him. Adrian wanted Dumas to tail her and get the goods on her so he could bargain with her before the divorce. Dumas was never able to find out who the boyfriend was before Adrian was killed."

"I'll be damned!" Mason said. "You think you've got all the pieces of the puzzle gathered up and all you have to do is fit them together and, suddenly, you discover that a whole lot of the pieces were missing all along."

He looked at Drake. "Is your man still watching Laurel's house?"

"He's there." Drake nodded. "I phoned him in his car right after I called you."

"Did he say anything about Latham? Had he gone?"

"He said Latham was still in the house."

"Let's go out there and see for ourselves what's going on," Mason said. "Do you think your buddy, Dumas, will notice that you've gone?"

"I already bade him good night. He won't miss me as long as his bottle holds out."

Outside the bar Mason and Drake got into their separate cars. Mason led the way, with Drake close behind him, up to the highway and the few miles along the highway to the beach house. Mason parked well behind where Drake's operative, Sam Baylor, was watching the house from his car. Mason had a clear view of the house, which was still lighted, and of Laurel's Lincoln parked in the driveway.

A couple of minutes passed and Drake opened the door on the passenger side of Mason's car and slid into the seat, closing the car door soundlessly.

Drake said, "I just talked to Sam Baylor over the car phone. I told him he could check out for the night after he told me Lieutenant Latham's still in the house."

"Been there a long time," Mason said, watching Baylor's car leave.

"You think she's told Latham anything?"

"Nothing he didn't already know." Mason was thoughtful for a moment before he added, "Well, now we know what the connection is between Adrian Gilbert's murder and the earlier murder of Martin Burress at the house up the street from the Adrian house. And now I know why I've had the feeling all along that Laurel's been concealing something; she's been trying to shield her boyfriend."

Drake interrupted. "Look, there's Latham coming out of the house now!"

They watched Latham cross the highway and head for a car parked several yards away.

"You think Lieutenant Latham suspected she had a boyfriend and that's why he's been tailing her, too?" Drake asked.

Mason leaned over and opened the car door nearest to Drake. "You can take off now, Paul. I'll see you in court in the morning. And I'm counting on having that exhibit ready. Right now I want to see where Lieutenant Latham's going. I want to have a little talk with him. Alone."

As Drake got out of the car, Mason added, "And, Paul, I don't think Latham suspected Laurel had a boyfriend. I think Latham *was* her boyfriend, and it started right after he first questioned her following the murder at the Burress house."

Mason grinned at the look of astonishment on Drake's face.

Mason drove away, keeping the taillights of Latham's car in sight, and reaching for the car phone.

He dialed Laurel's number and when she answered, he said, "Perry Mason, Laurel, I hope I'm not disturbing you."

"No, Mr. Mason, you're not. I've just been watching television, relaxing."

"Good," Mason said.

"Oh, Mr. Mason?"

"Yes?"

"I've been doing a lot of thinking and I really believe you should put me on the stand tomorrow, let me testify. I'm innocent. I'm sure I can convince the judge. I don't want this whole business to keep dragging on."

"We can talk about it in court tomorrow," Mason told her.

Mason disconnected the call. He had found out what he had wanted to know for sure: For whatever reason Latham had visited Laurel that night, it had nothing to do with the lieutenant's police investigation.

Up ahead, Latham's car had turned into the parking lot of the station house in the neighborhood of the Adrians' house in the hills. Mason waited in his car across the street until Latham entered the station house. Mason let several more minutes pass before he followed the lieutenant inside.

The desk sergeant in the front area of the station house said, "Yes, sir, can I help you?"

"I'd like a word with Lieutenant Latham if he's in. My name's Perry Mason. I'm an attorney. Lieutenant Latham knows me."

The desk sergeant used the phone and then nodded at Mason. "The lieutenant'll see you. Through that door and all the way to the back."

Latham was sitting at his desk when Mason reached the office. Latham stood, shook hands, and said, "Mr. Mason. I wouldn't have expected to see you. Not at this hour, at any rate."

"Looks like we're both working late," Mason said.

"Have a seat. What can I do for you?"

"A couple of questions I had," Mason said. "And I was in the neighborhood. I thought if you were here, I'd save time, talk with you tonight and maybe not have to question you in court tomorrow."

Latham looked perplexed. "I don't know what I'd have to say that I haven't already said. But, okay, go ahead."

"Specifically, that other murder case that occurred in the area, the murder of a man named Martin Burress, has been on my mind."

"In what way?"

Mason said, "Well, you were never able to solve it, I understand. And I wondered if there could have been a connection between the two murders, the murder of Adrian, the murder of Burress."

"Not that I know of, no connection we were able to establish."

"But you did put in a lot of work on the Burress case?" Mason persisted.

"I did, sure. Nothing ever came of it, though."

"I was told you questioned Mrs. Laurel Adrian a good many times directly after the Burress murder, isn't that right?"

"Mrs. Adrian and others," Latham said, rather quickly, Mason thought.

"Yes. But Mrs. Adrian in particular, so I've heard."

"I can't say her, in particular. As I recall, we talked to a good many people in the neighborhood."

"It was your questioning of Mrs. Adrian that made me wonder if perhaps, later, when her husband, too, was murdered you suspected a link between the two."

"No." Latham shook his head. "But even if we had it wouldn't have done us much good since we never got very far in our investigation of the first murder."

"You can understand that I have to try to look out for the best interests of my client," Mason said. "So I wonder, did you ever have any theories about who might have shot Mr. Burress?"

Latham seemed to relax. "The best we could come up with was that it was a random break-in and robbery and the victim walked in on it and was shot. Unofficially, most of us working on the case marked it down as probably the work of some drug user."

Mason nodded. "On the night of Gilbert Adrian's murder, when you questioned Mrs. Adrian at her house, didn't she ask you about the earlier murder?"

"As I recall, she did, yes."

"And that was when you told her that you remembered her from the times you talked to her about the Burress murder?"

Latham said, "I don't recall that precisely. Possibly that's the way it was."

"Now, on the night of Gilbert Adrian's murder, when you questioned Mrs. Adrian at her house, was there someone else present at all times during the questioning?"

Latham appeared surprised at the question. He said, "Yes, there was someone else present at all times, two patrolmen from here, as a matter of fact. Officers Spencer and Kohl."

Mason asked slowly, "So you never had a chance—so you were never alone with Mrs. Adrian from the time you reached the house and she was there?"

"I don't think I understand the point of your question. But, to repeat, there was someone else present at all times when I was with her. Why?"

Mason said lightly, "Let's just say I was checking to determine you were following proper procedure at all times. Looking out for my client's interest."

Mason stood, shook hands with Latham, and smiled. "Thank you for your time and cooperation, Lieutenant."

"You're welcome, Mr. Mason."

Mason started toward the door, stopped, and turned. "Oh, there is one other thing. That night, the night of Gilbert Adrian's murder, you were working the night shift?"

"Same as tonight, yes."

Mason said, "I don't think I ever asked you before: Were you here at the station house when the report of Adrian's murder came in? I suppose it's somewhere in the records around here?"

Latham hesitated a moment before he answered, "As a matter of fact, I was on my dinner break at the time."

"But still you got to the house quickly, almost ahead of the patrol cars, as I recall the court testimony."

"The report came in on my car radio and I responded."

"Yes. So you did. See you in court tomorrow, Lieutenant."

Mason closed the office door gently as he went out.

23

The atmosphere was tense and expectant in the crowded courtroom the next morning when Judge Moorman entered and took
his place on the bench and the pretrial hearing in the case of the
People versus Laurel Adrian resumed. The murder of Randolph
Adrian over the weekend had added a new element of sensation-
alism to the proceedings. Every seat in the courtroom was taken
and an overflow crowd filled the corridors outside the closed
doors.

Moments earlier Judge Moorman had summoned Perry Mason
and Carter Phillips to his chambers.

"Gentlemen," the judge admonished them, "I would hope we
can conclude this hearing swiftly today. I will not tolerate idle and
unnecessary wordplay between the two of you. I remind you
there is no jury present to impress. I hope I have made myself
clear."

Mason, with the judge's words still ringing in his ears, sat at the
defense table, knowing he faced a dilemma. Drake had not appeared with the exhibit Mason needed for his cross-examination
of the witness he wanted to call. Yet, Mason knew, Judge Moor-

man expected him to be ready to proceed with the defense's arguments. He could not stall.

Judge Moorman nodded to Mason.

"Call your witness."

Mason stood. He knew he had no choice other than what he was about to do.

"Your Honor," Mason said, "the defense calls Laurel Adrian."

Mason remained at the defense table as Laurel walked to the witness stand. He wanted everyone in court to have plenty of time to observe her alone and on her own while she was sworn in, and he even waited briefly after the ceremony before he stood and took his time walking toward the front of the court. It didn't hurt that everyone could see that she sat calm and composed as she awaited the opening of her testimony.

"Mrs. Adrian," Mason said, "you have heard the accounts given by the State's witnesses of the events of the night your husband, Gilbert Adrian, was shot."

"Yes."

"We're now going to go through the events of that night yet again so that we may all hear in your own words a description of what took place. You arrived home that evening at what time?"

"At approximately ten-thirty."

She went on quietly relating that she was surprised to see her husband's car parked at the house, and had hurried from her own car because she wanted to find out what was going on.

"I guess that's why I dropped the keys in the car. As I was on my way back to my car, the police came."

Mason stood to the side of the witness stand and asked her a series of questions that allowed her to relate how she had accompanied the police into the house, had found her husband dead, and though she was shocked and stunned, had been questioned by the police then and later at the station house.

In response to Mason's further questions, she explained how she had had dinner alone, started to drive to the beach house, as her husband had asked, and then turned around and come home again.

When she finished her account of that night, Mason felt she had done well in giving her explanation of what she had gone through.

"Turning to other matters," he said, "have you ever been married before?"

"No."

Mason led her through her story of her parents' deaths, of the business she had run, of her meeting with Gil Adrian and their marriage.

"Mr. Adrian had been married previously?"

"Yes. His wife died some years before he and I met."

"Mr. Adrian had a son by that marriage?"

"Yes. Randolph Adrian."

"Did you and Randolph Adrian ever have a misunderstanding?"

"I don't know that you could call it a misunderstanding. He made it clear that he didn't approve of my marriage to his father from the beginning."

"How did he make this clear to you?"

"He told me he believed I had married his father only for the money."

"Did you tell your husband what Randolph Adrian said to you?"

"Yes, I did. And Gil, my husband, told me to pay no attention. He said his son would probably have felt the same way about any woman he had married."

"Were you happy during your marriage?"

"For a time, yes. But then he, Gil, began to change and finally told me he wanted a divorce."

"Were you upset by this news?"

"At first, yes, I guess you could say that."

"But you had reconciled yourself to the divorce?"

"I had. For one thing, when stories began to appear in the news about his indictment—"

"Objection!" Carter Phillips said. "Immaterial."

Mason started to speak but Judge Moorman cut in quickly. "Overruled."

"Please continue," Mason said to Laurel.

"With all they were saying about him on the news, I began to wonder if I had ever really known him at all. He seemed not to be the same man I had married."

"So you had become reconciled to the divorce?"

"Yes."

"Did you have any knowledge that your husband planned to change his will?"

"No."

"Nor when he planned to change it?"

"No."

"Mrs. Adrian, do you have any knowledge of who shot and killed your husband?"

"No. I do not."

"Did you kill him?"

"I did not kill my husband," she answered.

"Thank you. I have no further questions."

Mason gave Laurel a reassuring smile as he walked away and Carter Phillips approached the witness stand.

"Mrs. Adrian," Phillips said, his voice harsh, "You and your husband were separated, is that correct?"

"Yes."

"And you were to be divorced?"

"Yes."

"And whose idea was the divorce?"

"His. It was his idea."

"Then I take it you didn't want the divorce?"

"I didn't suggest it; he did."

"But you didn't want it?"

"The divorce was his idea, yes. But I—we, that is, both of us agreed—"

"But it wasn't your idea?"

"He wanted us to separate, he wanted us to get a divorce but—"

"You told him you'd go along with it?"

"I guess—yes. But—"

"But you didn't really want to, or maybe you had other plans—?"

"No. I—"

"Objection!" Mason said. "The D.A. is stating facts—"

"Objection sustained."

Mason, seated again at the defense table, watched as Carter Phillips paused for a moment to look at the judge. Mason guessed the D.A. was trying to gauge the effect upon the judge of his tough cross-examination of Laurel.

He must have judged the effect to be positive, Mason assumed, because Phillips then began a barrage of quick, sharp-edged questions forcing Laurel to give answers about each and every incident of the night of the murder, from the moment she went into the house through her interrogation by Lieutenant Latham and Lieutenant Dallas at the police station house. From time to time Laurel grew confused. Mason tried to help by rising to object whenever he had the opportunity, and Phillips kept hammering away at her. And Mason was annoyed to see she had put on her dark sunglasses again.

"Have you ever seen this gun before?" Phillips held up the .38 that had been found on the desk in Gilbert Adrian's den.

"No." Laurel thought and added, "I mean I don't know, if you mean have I ever seen it before the night my husband was shot?"

"I didn't ask you that."

"I didn't understand—"

"Objection, Your Honor!" Mason said. "The witness is trying to explain she doesn't understand the question. Might the prosecution be instructed to rephrase the question?"

Phillips replied heatedly, "I don't need any instructions from the defense—"

"Gentlemen, please," Judge Moorman said. "Mr. Mason, I will instruct the prosecution when I find it necessary. Objection overruled. Mr. Phillips, you might want to clarify your question for the witness. Proceed."

Carter Phillips continued his cross-examination.

Mason tried to remain as objective as possible in trying to assess Laurel's performance on the witness stand and, sadly, had to conclude that with each question and answer she appeared more evasive. He glanced around the hushed courtroom and saw some of the familiar faces from earlier in the trial, Anselmo Costa's lawyer, Graham Kendrick, Steven Benedict, Margaret Starke, Lieutenant Latham, all gathered to watch the climax of the last day of the hearing.

"Perry!" a voice whispered into his ear. Mason glanced around. Drake eased into a chair. He was holding a large, upright parcel, enclosed in brown wrapping paper, that was larger than he was.

"Well?" Mason asked.

Drake grinned. "Here it is. Just the way you thought it would be."

"Good work, Paul. Damn good work!"

Mason turned his attention back to Laurel. It seemed to him she was all but cringing in the witness chair now.

In the front of the courtroom, Laurel was having difficulty as she tried to stammer out an answer to another of the D.A.'s hammering questions.

"I—I—don't—don't recall exactly—exactly what I said." She put a trembling finger up under her glasses as if to wipe away a tear. She was near collapse.

Carter Phillips snapped out his next questions.

"You were in your husband's den when he arrived home that night!"

"No."

"He found you at his desk. His safe was open. His papers were scattered everywhere. All your work!"

"No. It's not true—"

"He was in a rage. In the heat of anger he yanked out the gun he was carrying, a thirty-eight revolver, and fired two shots, missing you!"

"No! No! No."

Mason stood. "Objection!"

"Overruled."

The D.A. stood close to Laurel.

"You were panicked! You remembered the gun in the desk drawer, the thirty-two! Your gun! You grabbed for your gun. There was a struggle. The desk chair was overturned!"

"No—"

"Objection!" Mason was still standing.

"Overruled!"

Carter Phillips's next words echoed through the courtroom: "You shot and killed your husband, Gilbert Adrian, with two bullets through the brain!"

"Objection! Objection! Objection!"

The D.A. looked at Mason. "The prosecution has no further questions of this witness."

Laurel stepped down from the stand. She returned to the defense table.

"I'm sorry," she whispered to Mason. "I really made a mess of it, didn't I?"

"You did the best you could under the circumstances," he told her. "No one could ask you to do more."

"But I've lost the case for you, haven't I?"

"We'll see," Mason said. He thought of some words to leave with her. He said, " 'He that falls today may rise tomorrow.' That's a quote from *Don Quixote*."

Mason addressed the judge, "Your Honor, may I remind the court that there remains some incomplete testimony in this hearing. I refer to the prosecution's witnesses, Dr. James Lee and John Fallon. At the time they appeared for the People, I reserved the right to call them later. I respectfully ask to exercise that privilege now. I wish, first, to recall Dr. Lee."

When Mason had entered the courtroom a short while earlier he had made sure to check among the spectators that all the witnesses he had requested the court to order to be present this day were, in fact, there. He needed Dr. Lee and John Fallon back on the stand so he would have an excuse to introduce his new evidence.

Judge Moorman nodded his assent.

As Dr. Lee made his way to the witness stand, Mason added, "Your Honor, before questioning of this witness begins, may counsel approach the bench?"

"Come forward, Mr. Mason, Mr. Phillips."

Carter Phillips glared at Mason when they were both in front of the judge.

"Your Honor," Mason said, his voice barely above a whisper, "because of the nature of the testimony I hope and expect to elicit from the next witnesses, the defense now asks that this courtroom be sealed and that no one be allowed to leave or enter until the defense rests."

"What's this all about?" Phillips sputtered indignantly.

Judge Moorman's eyebrows were raised. "Mr. Mason, are you absolutely certain this action is necessary?"

"I am, Your Honor."

"Very well, request granted."

The judge announced to the courtroom that there would be a brief five-minute recess and that those present were to remain seated.

The judge stepped down and disappeared through the door to his chambers.

Mason returned to the defense table. Laurel looked at him anxiously. "What's happening, Mr. Mason?"

"Be patient," Mason said to her gently.

Della had entered the courtroom and come to the defense table. She handed Mason a photostat of a check, a photostat he had had subpoenaed from Randolph Adrian's bank that morning, of check number 324, which had been cashed.

Mason glanced at the check, winked at Della, and put the photostat into his coat pocket.

Several minutes passed. There was an air of expectancy in the room although Mason noticed that very few of the spectators were aware of what was happening as more marshals, in plain clothes, slipped into court, one by one, and took up positions ringing the entire room.

Judge Moorman returned and reminded the witness, Dr. James Lee, that he was still under oath, and Mason strode purposefully toward him.

"Dr. Lee, you have testified that the victim, Gilbert Adrian, was killed by two bullets that penetrated his skull and that both bullets remained inside the skull. Is that correct?"

"Yes, it is."

Mason turned toward the judge. "Your Honor, I would like now to introduce another exhibit into evidence."

"Proceed."

Mason beckoned to Drake who came forward lugging along the large paper-wrapped parcel.

Mason indicated the spot where the parcel was to be placed and Drake carefully unwrapped and removed the brown paper. There was a collective gasp from the spectators in the courtroom as the exhibit was revealed to be a life-size photographic cutout of the figure so familiar—the shaggy gray beard, gray hair, Stetson hat, and tinted aviator glasses—from pictures on TV and in the newspapers.

"*I object!*" Carter Phillips all but screamed out the shrill words.

"I object to the cheap theatrics of the defense, dragging this likeness of the victim into this court!"

"Your Honor," Mason said reasonably, "if I'm allowed to continue, it will soon become apparent that I have a sincere motive for introducing this exhibit into the proceedings."

"I will allow you a certain leeway, Mr. Mason," Judge Moorman said. "Objection overruled."

Mason turned the photographic cutout slightly so it directly faced the judge.

"Dr. Lee," he said, "would you please step down and indicate to the court, using this photographic likeness, the spots where the bullets entered Gilbert Adrian's brain?"

Dr. Lee moved quickly, taking a pen from his inside coat pocket. He pointed with the pen at the center of the forehead and a spot between the eyes in the photograph. "Here. And here."

"We have had testimony," Mason said, "that the body was found lying on the floor. Since the autopsy showed that both bullets remained inside the cranium, as you have testified, my question to you is, is it possible for you to state where Gilbert Adrian might have been standing in the room when he was shot?"

"The answer, Mr. Mason, is that it is impossible to determine that fact."

"No further questions. Thank you, Doctor." Mason turned to Phillips. "Your witness."

The D.A. shook his head. "No questions."

Dr. Lee walked away and the judge suggested to Mason that he call the next witness he had reserved to question.

John Fallon, manager of the Oaks Restaurant, who had been the opening prosecution witness, appeared slightly apprehensive as he took the witness stand for the second time.

As Mason approached Fallon, he held in his hands a copy of the duplicate appointment book Megan Calder, Gilbert Adrian's secretary, had found in the dead man's desk. Mason had left in place the life-size photographic cutout just used by Dr. Lee to demonstrate the places where the two bullets had been fired into Gilbert Adrian's head. Mason stood beside the figure as he asked his questions of the witness.

"Mr. Fallon, the testimony you have given in this trial as to the

time you say Mr. Adrian entered your restaurant and left is one of
the key elements the court must assess in determining the guilt or
innocence of the defendant, you do understand that?"

"Yes, sir." Fallon was watching Mason intently.

"You do understand the importance of your testimony?" Mason
persisted. "That if you are correct about the time, it would have
been impossible for the victim to have left the restaurant, to have
reached his house, emptied his safe and desk of papers, and then
to have been killed. All dependent upon your accuracy of the
time he arrived and departed from the restaurant."

"I understand, yes," Fallon said.

"So, I will ask you again, what time did Gilbert Adrian arrive at
your restaurant and what time did he leave on the night of May
eleventh?"

John Fallon was more at ease as he answered, "Mr. Adrian came
in at nine P.M. and left at approximately nine-forty-five P.M. on
the night of May eleventh."

"And while he was there, he used the pay telephone to make a
call?"

"Yes, sir. He did."

Mason asked his next question slowly. "Are you certain, Mr.
Fallon, that at the time Mr. Adrian was in your restaurant, he had
no scratches or marks on his face? I don't believe I heard you offer
such testimony."

Fallon raised his voice to make it clear he was positive on the
point. "No, sir. There were no marks or scratches on his face.
None."

"You observed him closely that night?" Mason asked quickly.
"You were as close to him that night as you are to me now?"

"As close, probably closer."

Mason indicated the photographic cutout figure. "And there
were no more scratches or marks on his face than there are on the
face of this photographic likeness?"

"None! No!" Fallon answered emphatically. "His face looked
just like it does there."

"Of course it did," Mason agreed. He turned away from Fallon
and took a step to one side, saying, "We have had testimony
regarding the duplicate appointment book Gilbert Adrian kept

hidden secretly away in his desk drawer at the office." Mason held up the book. He shook his head. "So much concealment in this case. And now is the time to uncover the truth."

Mason reached out with his free hand toward the cutout figure beside him that he had instructed Drake to have made.

The composite picture had been easy to assemble in the photographic studio Drake had gone to for help. Separate photographs had been reproduced and blown up to lifesize of two figures who were of equal height and weight. One of the photographs was of Gilbert Adrian with his shaggy gray beard, gray hair showing under his Stetson hat, the tinted aviator glasses covering his eyes. In the photographic studio, the beard, hair, hat, and glasses had been cut out with a razor blade from Adrian's picture and had been mounted and held in place with artist's rubber cement upon the face in the second photograph.

Only by this process of transposing had it been possible to show how the man in the second photograph, who was now clean-shaven and short-haired and who no longer wore the hat and glasses, had looked on the night of May 11.

Mason said, "One of the biggest problems in the case has been that the evidence, the physical evidence, that would have proved who the killer of Gilbert Adrian was had been destroyed. Permanently, so the killer thought. And that physical evidence had to be restored."

Mason quickly peeled away the superimposed beard, hair, hat, and glasses, revealing the face underneath. "This," he said, "is the man who was at the Oaks Restaurant, who shot the unidentified man in the doorway of the place."

There was confusion in the courtroom as several marshals rushed forward and surrounded a man who had bolted from his seat and tried to make a dash for the rear doors.

Carter Phillips had half risen from his chair to watch, spectators were craning their heads to see what was going on, and Judge Moorman had lifted his gavel and held it suspended in midair.

Perry Mason pointed to the man being restrained by the marshals. "That man there!" he announced in a loud voice.

The judge pounded his gavel to quiet the courtroom.

Mason went on talking. "It was Steven Benedict, hired for the job because with the right-length hair and beard, the hat and glasses, he was virtually a dead ringer for Adrian, who was at the restaurant! At the same time it was Gilbert Adrian who was at his own house, in his den, clearing out his safe and desk and, incidentally, picking up his passport as he prepared to skip the country the next morning before he was due to appear in court."

In the middle of the courtroom Steven Benedict was struggling with the marshals, trying to break free. It took six marshals to restrain and handcuff him.

There were exclamations of surprise from some of the spectators in the courtroom and Judge Moorman pounded his gavel.

"Your Honor! Your Honor!" Carter Phillips was shouting above the din in the room. "The prosecution requests a continuance until tomorrow morning."

"Very well," Judge Moorman said, "the court will reconvene at ten A.M. tomorrow."

Mason saw Carter Phillips and Lieutenant Ray Dallas conferring, then Dallas crossed to the marshals who were restraining Steven Benedict. Phillips joined Dallas and followed the marshals as they led Benedict away to hold him for questioning.

Mason motioned to Paul Drake, Jr., and Della to escort Laurel Adrian from the courtroom. Drake took the photographic cutout exhibit with him.

Lieutenant Dallas, grim-faced, approached Mason as Judge Moorman left the bench, the news reporters covering the trial hurried to telephones, and the spectators slowly moved out of the courtroom.

"I sure as hell hope you know what you're doing," Dallas said bitingly to Mason.

"What I'm doing, Ray," Mason said easily, "is preparing to offer you evidence to prove who murdered Gilbert Adrian *and* Randolph Adrian, as well. But of course it will be you, the police, who will use the evidence to solve the crimes."

"All right, let's talk."

The two men walked in silence to a small conference room a few doors away from the judge's chambers off a corridor at the front of the courtroom.

Mason sat in one of the hard wooden armchairs. Ray Dallas

perched on a corner of the small conference table, and said, "All right, Counselor. Let's hear it."

Mason held up the appointment book. "The significance of this secret appointment book Adrian kept is that the notations he made in parentheses were the appointments attended by his double, Steven Benedict. Most of those appointments were of minor importance, occasions where only an appearance was necessary. As a matter of fact I have here that newspaper photo supposedly made of Gilbert Adrian at a ground-breaking ceremony on April twenty-second. Yet we had testimony in this courtroom from Councilwoman Janet Coleman that Gilbert Adrian was in Las Vegas on that day. So, using a double did allow Adrian himself a certain amount of freedom to be elsewhere. Also—"

Mason paused to put down the appointment book. "—Adrian *did* know that he had made a lot of enemies and sooner or later one of them might try to do away with him, which brings us to the night of May eleventh. That night Adrian was supposed to meet with a representative of Anselmo Costa's at the Oaks Restaurant. In time it will, I'm sure, be established as a fact that Costa and Adrian were involved in money laundering and bribery. And Costa, fearing Adrian might talk at the trial that was to begin the next day, sent a hit man to silence him."

Mason was pleased that Dallas had begun to take notes. "Adrian must have had a hunch what was going to happen, so he sent our friend, Steven Benedict," Mason continued. "The call at the pay phone in the restaurant was of course made by Benedict, calling his own house. So, at the restaurant Benedict, after talking with the hit man, must have realized he had been set up for execution by Adrian, in place of Adrian. As they were leaving, Benedict got the drop on the other man, shot him and then went after Adrian. Benedict walked in on Adrian, fired the last two shots from the thirty-eight revolver he was carrying, and missed, the shots burying themselves in the wall of the den. Adrian had been searching the desk and had seen Laurel's gun in the drawer. He tried to get to the gun, the thirty-two revolver. There was a struggle and Benedict got possession of the gun. Steven Benedict shot and killed Gilbert Adrian, took the money from the open safe, and got away before Laurel Adrian and the police reached the house. Benedict had wiped away his own fingerprints and put the thirty-two revolver back into the desk drawer. That's what happened."

Mason rubbed the bridge of his nose, and said softly, "You see, Benedict had solid motives for killing Adrian. One, Adrian had set him up to be killed, and two—and perhaps most important—Benedict reasoned that Adrian was the only one who could know that it was he, Benedict, who shot the man at the Oaks Restaurant. Once Benedict shed the beard, the glasses, the Stetson hat, he thought he was free and clear."

"All right, Perry," Dallas said. "It hangs together, I have to hand it to you."

"Thanks, Ray." Mason took the photostat of Randolph Adrian's check from his pocket and handed it to Dallas. "Incidentally, you might find this handy to have when you prosecute Benedict for the second murder, the murder of Randolph Adrian. Benedict cashed it this morning."

Dallas asked, "You figure Randolph Adrian knew that Benedict had killed his father?"

Mason shrugged. "Hard to say. Randolph had the newspaper and was going to show it to Laurel. That's why he called her and asked her to come to his house. Randolph must have been listening when Janet Coleman testified Gilbert Adrian was in Las Vegas on April twenty-second and he remembered something about that date—about the ground-breaking ceremony—where supposedly Gilbert Adrian was photographed. And he found an old copy of the newspaper to prove his father couldn't be in two places at once. Randolph probably hoped to help Laurel and make a settlement on the will. I don't think Benedict knew about any of this."

"That's my theory, too," Dallas said. "Benedict went to Randolph's house to pick up a check."

"And," Mason nodded, "I think Benedict had it in mind, when Randolph told him that night that Laurel was coming by, he'd set Laurel up again by killing Randolph so it would look like she did it. That way it would direct suspicion away from him in Gilbert Adrian's murder, if by chance she was freed of killing her husband."

Lieutenant Dallas stood. "Okay, we'll confront Steven Benedict with the evidence and see if we can crack him."

"With your skill," Mason said, "I have no doubt that you will have the pleasure of nailing him—and the credit—and tomorrow Carter Phillips will be able to dismiss the charges against Laurel Adrian."

24

When court reconvened the next morning at ten o'clock, Carter Phillips stood before the bench.

"Your Honor," he said, "the prosecution has a startling statement to make in these proceedings, if the court please."

Judge Moorman nodded. "Proceed."

"Overnight," the D.A. said, "the L.A.P.D.—especially Lieutenant Raymond Dallas—has assembled new and conclusive evidence in the investigation of the murder of Gilbert Adrian. As a result of this new evidence, the police have a videotaped confession from Steven Benedict admitting his sole complicity in the homicide shooting of Gilbert Adrian. It is my understanding that Your Honor has viewed this videotape in chambers earlier this morning."

"I have." Judge Moorman nodded his head.

"Under the circumstances," Carter Phillips said, "the prosecution moves to dismiss the case against the defendant in this hearing, Laurel Adrian."

The D.A. stepped back and sat down.

Judge Moorman, clearly trying to suppress a smile, directed his next remark to Perry Mason. "Does the defense have any objections, Mr. Mason?"

Mason smiled openly. "No objections, Your Honor. No objections at all."

Judge Moorman banged his gavel. "The case against the defendant, Laurel Adrian, is dismissed. She is free to leave forthwith. This court is adjourned."

At the defense table Laurel Adrian threw her arms around Perry Mason's neck. "Oh! Thank you so much, Mr. Mason."

Mason grinned. A crowd of spectators formed around them to offer congratulations. Della and Drake pushed through the crowd. Della shook Mason's hand and Drake pounded him on the back.

Ray Dallas walked up. He was smiling. "Nice going, Counselor. You sure pulled the rabbit out of the hat this time—and out of the beard and aviator glasses."

"You contributed your share of the work, Ray," Mason said. "Was it hard to get him to confess?"

Dallas shook his head. "The evidence had him boxed in on all sides. The clincher was that once he had killed the guy at the Oaks Restaurant he had to kill Gilbert Adrian who was the only one, he assumed, who could tie him to that killing. In some ways Benedict was just a guy who got in over his head and couldn't figure out how to save himself." Dallas paused and added, "But then, that's true of most people who commit murder and try to get away with it."

"On that we agree," Mason said.

Dallas patted him on the shoulder. "See you around, Perry," he said and walked away.

Drake came rushing up and grabbed Mason by the arm. "Come on, we have to go."

"What's the hurry?" Mason asked.

"You'll see."

Drake, Della, Mason, and Laurel pushed through the crowd and outside. Mason and Laurel smiled for the cameras and Drake hurried them to the waiting car.

Mason still didn't know what all the rush was about and Drake wouldn't tell him until the car stopped and they were all inside Mason's favorite restaurant, Clay's Bar and Grill.

The whole place had been festooned with colorful balloons and there was a table set up with glasses and buckets of chilled champagne. In addition to Della, Drake, Mason, and Laurel, there were also present Megan Calder, Janet Coleman, Melanie Sandford, and Drake's investigator, Joe Lennart. Drake, knowing what Mason proposed to do in court that day and certain of success, had made all the arrangements with Della's help. Those who were invited were the ones who had helped or encouraged Laurel's defense.

The champagne was poured and toasts were drunk as the group mingled around the room.

Laurel came over and kissed Mason's cheek, saying she was leaving. They were alone at the table for a moment and Mason said confidentially, "Laurel, can I ask you a question?"

"Yes. Sure. Anything."

"I always had a feeling you hadn't told me everything in this case. Was I right?"

She looked at him keenly. "You were right. The night of the murder when I arrived home I went into the house before the police got there. I saw that Gil had been shot and was dead. I ran back outside and that's when the police came. I don't think I ever fooled them about the keys though. The police, I mean. I think they knew I palmed them out of my handbag on the way to the car. They just never pressed me on the point."

She smiled wryly. "I was afraid if I told them I had been in the house already they would be positive I had killed him with his gun. But I want you to know I never committed perjury on this point. I was never asked this question directly and I never directly denied it under oath."

Mason frowned at her sternly. She flushed and looked away.

"I will say," she added, "that I think that's why I failed the polygraph test, as I suspected I did."

"And I suspect for another reason, too," Mason suggested softly. "You were trying to protect Frank Latham."

She was startled. "You knew about him?"

"Yes. At first, the night Gilbert Adrian was killed, you couldn't be sure Latham hadn't done it, could you?"

"I—" she shook her head, "no. I didn't think so but Frank and I had no chance to talk alone. Later, I wanted to protect him because if people knew about us, they'd think I was the reason Frank killed Gil, or Frank was the reason I killed Gil."

"That's another reason why you got away with the business about going to the car and finding the keys, isn't it? Frank Latham was protecting you on your story," Mason said.

"You guessed it again." Laurel looked at him wide-eyed. "Frank was right behind me when I went back to the car to pretend to look for the keys. He probably saw what I was doing. But since he was directly in back of me he blocked the view the other police there might have had. I was so scared that night I hardly knew what I was doing. What I did know was I hadn't killed Gil."

She thought for a moment and then said, "Frank always knew I could never have killed Gil. He knew it but he was helpless to do anything about saving me. We talked about it, when we were finally able to get together alone after the night it happened. He wanted to come forward, declare himself and his love for me. But both of us were sure it would only make things worse for me. He didn't care about himself but it was an agonizing dilemma for him."

"Your relationship with Latham started right after that murder at the Burress house, didn't it?"

She nodded. "Frank and I were very much attracted to one another. Frank was afraid for me, living with Gil. But, as attracted to one another as we were—as we are still—we decided not to let our relationship develop beyond seeing one another as often as we could. I knew Gil and I were divorcing so Frank and I decided we could wait. I want you to know that."

"Okay," Mason said again. "I'm satisfied. I wish you and Frank Latham good luck."

When Laurel was gone, Della came to sit for a moment with Mason.

"Would you take me for an early dinner tonight, Perry?"

"Sure," he said. "Paul, too?"

She shook her head. "No. Just us."

Drake brought over a champagne bottle and filled Mason's glass.

"Now, Perry," Drake said, "let's hear how you reasoned the whole case out."

Mason took a sip of champagne as the others drew quiet and listened.

"The first time you and I saw Steven Benedict, Paul, I noticed how sunburned his face was, as if he hadn't been outdoors for a long time, or as if his face had been covered from the sun. Then there was the fact that nobody ever remembered seeing him around although he was supposed to be Adrian's bodyguard. Even Laurel couldn't remember seeing him although she thought he looked familiar. But the real tip-off came—"

Mason paused to take another sip of champagne. "—one night when they were doing a summary of the trial on TV and I had the sound turned down. They were showing those stupid sketches that artist does in the courtroom, where everybody looks like they have beards. And I saw this one person and I thought it was a sketch of Gilbert Adrian. Only of course it wasn't; Gilbert Adrian was never in court.

"I didn't realize what I had seen until later and I suspected then that the person I had seen was Benedict. And later there was the business of the newspaper photograph and the double-entry appointment book. So I thought to have the photographic cutout made. If Benedict was the killer, then all the worrisome pieces in the case, the time element particularly, fell into place."

"Well, you were right," Drake said. He asked another question. "I always wondered, from the beginning of the case, though, how you could be so sure Laurel was innocent—with all the evidence there was against her."

"I simply applied 'Occam's razor' to the situation." Mason smiled.

"Whose razor?" Drake asked.

"Occam's razor," Mason explained. "William of Occam was a fourteenth-century philosopher. And Occam's razor, as it came to be called, was a theory he had that the simplest of competing explanations in a given situation should be preferred to the more complex. To put it more plainly, that the simplest explanation in a given situation is most likely the correct explanation. A friend of mine, New York City Police Captain John O'Shea, first told me of Occam's razor. In the case of Laurel Adrian, with all the other people who wanted Gilbert Adrian dead, the simplest explanation to me was that she should be given the benefit of the doubt."

"I got it," Drake said. "It sure makes sense when you put it that way."

Mason grinned. "Even in a case where there are too many murders."